697

D1005244

# Once Removed

# Once Removed

A novel by

**Andrew Unger**

TURNSTONE PRESS

Once Removed
copyright © Andrew Unger 2020
Turnstone Press
Artspace Building
206-100 Arthur Street
Winnipeg, MB
R3B 1H3 Canada
www.TurnstonePress.com

All rights reserved. No part of this book may be reproduced or
transmitted in any form or by any means—graphic, electronic or
mechanical—without the prior written permission of the publisher. Any
request to photocopy any part of this book shall be directed in writing to
Access Copyright, Toronto.

Turnstone Press gratefully acknowledges the assistance of the Canada
Council for the Arts, the Manitoba Arts Council, the Government of
Canada through the Canada Book Fund, and the Province of Manitoba
through the Book Publishing Tax Credit and the Book Publisher
Marketing Assistance Program.

Cover: Mennonite pattern on canvas floor cloth by Margruite Krahn,
inspired by Sara Janzen, Neuhorst, MB. c. 1920s.

Printed and bound in Canada by Friesens.

Library and Archives Canada Cataloguing in Publication

Title: Once removed / a novel by Andrew Unger.
Names: Unger, Andrew, 1979- author.
Identifiers: Canadiana (print) 20200235133 | Canadiana (ebook)
    2020023532X | ISBN 9780888017093 (softcover) | ISBN
    9780888017109 (EPUB) | ISBN 9780888017116 (Kindle) |
    ISBN 9780888017123 (PDF)
Classification: LCC PS8641.N44 O53 2020 | DDC C813/.6—dc23

MANITOBA ARTS COUNCIL
CONSEIL DES ARTS DU MANITOBA

Canada Council    Conseil des arts
for the Arts      du Canada

Funded by the Government of Canada
Financé par le gouvernement du Canada

Canada

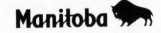

Manitoba

*for Erin*
*and*
*for the historians, writers, and preservers of memory*

The following words—every jot and tittle—are a work of fiction, or as my ancestors would say, this book "is complete and utter *dommheit*." As such, it would be a foolhardy and futile endeavour to scour these pages for allusions to real people, places, or events—even the history referenced herein is treated fictionally. Any resemblance to your Uncle Henry or Aunt Martha is a coincidence and should not instigate nasty emails or excommunication proceedings.

# Once Removed

# Somma

# One

They cut down twenty trees by the Co-op this week. Elms. They claimed they were diseased and marked each one with a red dot just hours before the Thiessen boys came with their chainsaws. The whole time I sat there in the truck with the engine idling and the radio tuned to the funeral announcements, waiting for Mr. Vogt to pound on the hood a couple times and say, "*Na*, Timothy, looks like you're good to go." Then I hauled it all off to the dump to be burned.

It wasn't a pleasant scene, all those trees coming down and the barren land left there afterwards, but I did have some reason to be optimistic. The last time a whole row of trees went down like this, there was a liquor store on the cleared lot within months. It's our first one and, rumour has it, the busiest in rural Manitoba. Now we don't have to sneak off to Ste. Adèle for booze. We can get our wine-in-a-box right here in Edenfeld. Another patch of elms was declared diseased to make way for a dollar store. Progress is progress. Katie and I have a beautiful mature tree in our backyard too, but thankfully it's behind the house and therefore in an undesirable location for commercial enterprise. I worry about those tall ones on Wilshire, though. They're oaks, remnants of a large stand that predates European settlement in this area. There's a plaque nearby stating as much, which appears to have protected them from the ambitions of local land developers and/or mayors who also happen to be land developers.

I asked Mr. Vogt about the land by the Co-op, if he knew what was happening to it, but all he said was, "Mayor's orders," and he left the rest to my imagination. I'm not sure that was a good idea, because I can envision some pretty awful things cropping up on that lot. Probably another donut shop with inadequate drive-through space. Mr. Vogt says it's better not to ask too many questions.

Edenfeld prides itself on our aggressive disease prevention program, which requires the swift removal of trees that are past their prime and buildings that, in Mr. Vogt's words, "attract vermin if left to their own devices." These are the very same trees and buildings that other towns might try to preserve for environmental or historical reasons. According to the sign on the highway, Edenfeld was founded in 1876, but good luck finding anything older than about 1990. There are some exceptions, of course, but the Parks and Rec department is rapidly making them a thing of the past.

Once things seemed under control at the Co-op, Mr.

Vogt tasked me with picking the dandelions at BLT Wiens Memorial Park. BLT Wiens is actually still alive and still our mayor, but the town figured it would be more economical to include the word "Memorial" right away rather than waiting to add it in later. I was told to pick the weeds by hand, and with the three Thiessens busy felling the last of the trees, the job was mine alone. Chemical herbicides are banned in our province, a recent law that greatly upset Edenfeld politicians who feel that "weeding is a strictly civic matter." BLT explained all this in an angry memo that, for some reason, also specified that we couldn't even use citrus juice to kill the weeds, but I think that had less to do with the environmental impact and more to do with maintaining our thriving local potluck scene, which has always relied on an ample supply of lemon meringue pie, among other varieties. The new weeding process is much more labour-intensive, such that the mayor's eponymous park is the only one in town that receives this level of attention.

Mr. Vogt said I should bring my chainsaw.

"Not for the dandelions, of course," he clarified, "but if you see an elm that looks iffy, go for it!" He always speaks a little louder than necessary, which makes him a suitable candidate to run a demolition crew, but not someone to chat with for prolonged periods in the church lobby.

I didn't get all the dandelions picked, but by the end of the work day I had more than enough to fill a pail for Mr. Harder. I was supposed to meet him after work at Ernie's Diner above the gas station. I figured I could spare a pail of dandelions, since Mr. Harder's wine-making supply is always running low and he's one of my favourite clients.

I've been working on his family history book for a while now.

Katie and I are hoping that eventually I can transition to writing full-time, but at the moment the Parks and Rec job pays the bills. My friend Randall says my life is "fraught with cognitive dissonance." He admits his is too, only for reasons that he never fully articulates, but which I assume have something to do with the fact that he's unmarried and well into his thirties and the pressure is on from his mother to do something about that situation.

I'm a ghostwriter—or trying to be, anyway. This means I write books for other people. So does Randall. We're guns for hire, so to speak, though around here gun analogies are generally frowned upon. As much as I'd prefer to spend my days preserving the memories of Edenfeld's senior citizens, rather than demolishing heritage buildings to create space for yet another strip mall, I simply can't afford that luxury. I have a mortgage to pay and a wife who's finishing her master's in contemporary philosophy and there isn't enough ghostwriting work to keep both Randall and me employed full-time.

"Not yet," Katie always says.

Mr. Harder is into trees too. There's one right outside the manor where he lives that is said to be a descendant of the Great Oak of Chortitza. It was planted by Edenfeld's pioneers using seeds they brought from the old country. Sometimes, when the weather is nice, we sit on the porch swing at the manor and he never fails to point it out and say, "That tree over there, Timothy, is *frindschauft* of the famous Great Oak." He asked me to dedicate an entire chapter to the Great Oak of Chortitza. I felt it was a bit much for only one tree, but he insisted. He travelled to Russia and Ukraine in the nineties on one of those Mennonite history tours where he took dozens of photos of the famous Great Oak, including at least a couple that weren't completely out of focus. He wants to include about thirty pages' worth in his book. "It'll be the most comprehensive visual documentation of the Great Oak ever put into print," he boasted. I assured him that even at one or two pages he'd still have the record.

"When I went there," said Mr. Harder, "there weren't more than a handful of branches that still had green leaves on them."

He showed me a snapshot that confirmed his assessment.

"It looks dead," I observed.

"Oh, it's not dead," he assured me. "Just dying."

I told him its prospects were about as good as any of the trees here in Edenfeld. He laughed. He gets me. I guess that's why he hired me to ghostwrite his latest book for him. It's tentatively titled *The Harder Path: Problems and How We Overcame Them from Molotschna to Southern Manitoba* by Dietrich F. Harder. The book is the third in a series after *Working Hard and Praying Harder: Life on the Farm* and a slim volume that documents his father's declining years called *You Know, Quite Frankly, It's Never Been Harder.* Randall wrote that one.

A large chunk of Mr. Harder's new book is based on the notes he took during that trip to Eastern Europe twenty-five years ago, only his recollection of the facts is rather suspect and his spelling is all over the place. However, checking facts and correcting spelling are just two of the many services a ghostwriter can provide. That's what Randall and I always tell clients anyway, you know, to drum up business. Our mysterious ability to boot up a computer also seems to impress the locals, and we're some of the only people around here reasonably proficient with a word processor. This is a great embarrassment for the mayor, who considers himself a real progressive. For a while, he even offered a course at the library called "Computer Usage for Mennonites and Other Beginners," but only six people signed up and most of them were just in it for the free cheese curds and rolled up slices of processed ham the town provided for attendees. The event wasn't entirely useless; BLT used a photo of his students peering with bewilderment into their computer monitors for one of his campaign mailers.

I enjoy working with Mr. Harder, but it can be confusing at times. Over the centuries, the Harders lived in three different countries in three successive villages each called Edenfeld, a name that refers to the Garden of Eden, and one that's more blindly optimistic than accurate. Given the large number of villages Mennonites have christened with that name, I often have to clarify, "You mean Edenfeld, Russia, not Edenfeld, Canada, right?" and Mr. Harder isn't always sure, so sometimes we look at the photos and guess based on what people are wearing or how much snow has accumulated in front of the houses, but even then, it isn't always conclusive. There were Edenfelds all over the place in the old country, each one of them abandoned a long time ago. There used to be more than one here too. There was another Edenfeld on the other side of the river that was labelled on old maps as "Lower Edenfeld," probably because it was a few miles closer to the American border.

The whole town escaped to Paraguay long ago, where they hacked out rich farmland from dense jungle. Our Edenfeld is closer to the city, which means on weekends we escape to the mall and hack our way through dense crowds to get deals on yoga pants.

Mr. Harder also tends to mix up the Bolsheviks and Makhnovists and has real difficulty recalling what particular torture device was used against our people in what particular time period. "I don't think they used tongue screws in the Soviet Union," I recall telling him. But he replied, "Oh, yes, yes they did, to silence the heretics from preaching while they were being burned at the stake." His timeline is often way off.

When five o'clock rolled around, I took my dandelions and went over to the diner for our meeting. I have an ongoing arrangement with Ernie to save the table that overlooks the street so I can observe the locals and document their idiosyncrasies for future writing projects. Since Ernie very much appreciates the volume of *plautz* I consume, he's willing to reserve this prime spot for me. He even puts one of those triangular signs at the edge of the table that says "Reserved for a Valued Customer," which is usually covered in grease and always makes me feel appreciated.

When I arrived that day, however, the greasy sign wasn't there and I saw that Ernie had given my spot to City Sheila, who has lived in Edenfeld for two full decades, but has maintained this nickname due to her English surname and liberal use of eyeliner. Ernie apologized to me and said he would ask Sheila to move. It was a simple oversight—no big deal—but Ernie seemed quite eager to move Sheila to another spot. I imagine he didn't want her well-made-up face, with her fiery red lipstick, greeting customers as they approached the building. She sells cosmetics from the trunk of her car, and the fact that her ostentatious pink convertible was parked in Ernie's lot was probably not to his liking either. He spoke to her in Plautdietsch and she had no clue what the man was blathering on about, but with me standing there awkwardly and Ernie flapping his arms, she must have gathered there was an issue.

It was an issue for Ernie anyway. I told them both that it was fine and I'd find another table, but by then City Sheila was already standing with her cutlery in hand, ready to move, and I felt terrible about the whole situation.

I asked her for a catalogue and promised I'd order a few nail files and a cuticle trimmer for Katie.

"I feel awful about this," I said in English. "I really didn't need the table."

City Sheila sighed. "It's no problem," she said. "I know how Ernie can get."

I sat down and ordered a coffee and piece of rhubarb *plautz*, my favourite. I left the menu open in front of me in case I wanted to order more, the whole time wondering what on earth was keeping Mr. Harder. He was already twenty minutes late and that didn't even factor in the twenty minutes by which he was usually early. We were supposed to discuss his older brother David and the time he spent in the World War II Conscientious Objector camp out west. He claims David single-handedly built nine miles of the Trans-Canada Highway with nothing but a pickaxe and a shovel, including a stretch that went right on through the heart of the Rocky Mountains. Mr.

Harder even showed me a piece of rock that he'd kept as a memento all these years. "Blasted straight through that mountain, he did." This was yet another story that could probably use a fact check.

I glanced down to the street below, anticipating Mr. Harder's arrival. The server with the tongue piercing came to warm up my coffee, even though I'd hardly touched it. She's new; one of Ernie's nieces he's trying to persuade to stay in Edenfeld by offering her a few hours at the diner and turning a blind eye to her perforated tongue. When she saw that the cup was still full, she raised an eyebrow and asked if there was something wrong with it. I said it was fine and smiled, trying to be pleasant. For a moment, I considered making a comment about her mouth jewelry, but quickly thought better of it. The urge to make small talk with strangers is something I have to suppress and, thankfully, at my age I still can, but I'm sure in twenty or thirty years I'll be the guy chatting up the server. "So, Rebecca," I'll say, leaning in to read her name tag. Then I'll tell her how her piercing reminds me of our distant ancestors who were tortured for their faith, and I'll ask her how it feels to have a piece of metal in her tongue and if it prevents her, in any way, from sharing the gospel. For now I kept quiet, though, and instead peered out the window to the street below, watching Edenfelders go about their daily lives.

It was hot that day, well above thirty, or what Mr. Harder would call ninety, but despite the near-suffocating temperature, Ernie was too cheap to turn on the AC. "Once it hits a hundred, then we'll talk." The windows were wide open and I could hear cars honking and cattle lowing in the distance. Is that the right word? Lowing? Whatever it's called, they were making the noise that cows tend to make when they're in distress or mating or whatever and, though I could not confirm it with my own eyes, I imagined that the two sounds, that of the cars and that of the cows, were somehow connected. The cars, I assumed, were honking *at* the cows, or the cows, perhaps, were expressing their displeasure at the traffic. Whenever a cow breaks free from its pasture, the Parks and Rec crew has to go out there and scoop manure off the street.

The corner of Sunset and Main is the commercial hub of town, or it once was anyway. However, since almost everyone does their shopping in the city these days, at one of those massive stores where they load the puffed wheat onto the back of your truck with a forklift, Edenfeld's Main Street is not nearly as bustling as you might expect. BLT is desperately hoping to attract exactly such a facility to Edenfeld, which will keep some of that puffed wheat money in town, he says. He's even constructed a new road called Megamart Way, which tends to confuse out-of-towners when they discover that it's nothing but wishful thinking at the moment. It does, however, lead to a very attractive ditch.

Down on the street, a jogger ran past, his head high and smiling like his favourite Phil Collins song had just come on through his headphones or he'd beat his personal best for most laps up and down Main Street. He ran on the spot for a while, waiting for the light to change, then carried on past a woman in a long floral dress who was rollerblading in front of the café. I wrote all this down. The rollerblading woman stopped to chat in Plautdietsch with another woman in a similar dress who was wearing white sneakers instead of rollerblades and so seemed very short in comparison. Both were wearing headscarves. The rollerblading one seemed upset about something and was speaking sternly and using her height advantage to tower over the other woman. I wasn't sure what exactly they were arguing about, but I gathered from the frequent use of the word *"heena"* that it had something to do with chickens. I didn't want to lean too close to the window, though, because even though my Plautdietsch isn't that great, I didn't want them to know I was listening. Instead, I gazed into the distance, like I was looking past them at that huge stack of cabbages across the street at Frugal Frank's Groceries and More, but I kept writing what I could glean from their interaction. I record details like this in my notebook hoping that if I ever write my own book, and not just other people's stories, this material might be of some value.

When the server in the kerchief, not the one with the pierced tongue, came up and asked me what I was writing and if I'd like a hot bowl of *borscht* or maybe a lovely *schnetje* with strawberry jam, I said I was fine and that I was writing an obituary notice, which was the most plausible answer I could conjure at the moment. I didn't want to reveal my penchant for eavesdropping on the locals.

"Oh, I'm sorry to hear that. Was it someone close to you?"

I nodded and she offered to pray for me even though I said it wasn't necessary. She kept it brief, reciting something from memory, presumably because there was a table full of elderly women in red hats who needed her attention.

When Mr. Harder finally showed up, I greeted him

from the window, then readied my notes as he made his way up the stairs. I had brought along a stack of history books and a few issues of *Preservings*. I figured this stuff would be useful source material for our project. I'd done a lot of research. I even got my hands on *The Harder Book,* which was packed with genealogies and baptismal records and maiden names of each and every person in the family tree since the mid-eighteenth century. Each Harder family has their own book because, as I'm sure you know, not all Harders are closely related. Some came in the 1870s fleeing the tsar and some came in the 1920s fleeing the people who replaced the tsar. Some are *jantsied* Harders and some are *ditsied* Harders and some are from the mysterious Scratching River settlement. There are even the Mexico Harders and a few branches of those too. This particular volume was thick and brown and embossed with gold lettering that said "Descendants of Heinrich B. Harder and Anna R. Funk (1723-1980)." It was the hardcover edition.

You can tell a lot about the relative stature of an Edenfeld family by examining the quality of binding used in their family history books, a practice that has continued despite stern admonishment from local churches. According to Reverend Broesky, hardcover bindings are a symbol of worldly pride. "How presumptuous!" he exclaimed. "These books are not the Bible. There is no need for these stories to be preserved for all eternity. No, brothers and sisters, in most cases a simple Xerox on the church copier will be more than sufficient." Despite the warning, many Edenfeld families continue to showcase their status with hardcover bindings. The Harders, the evidence would suggest, are among our more prominent citizens.

It took Mr. Harder a while to get up the stairs, even after Ernie went down to give him a hand. When they entered the room a few minutes later, Mr. Harder had Ernie firmly gripped at the elbow and they were muttering to each other in our language and it seemed that neither man was too pleased with how the other one was handling matters. I stood to greet Mr. Harder. He was well dressed, as always, with a clean collared shirt, pressed pants, and a brand new pair of black suspenders. He waved enthusiastically, buoyed by Ernie's ability to keep him upright, then shuffled towards me. I shoved the bucket of dandelions out of the way with my foot so he wouldn't trip over it.

"*Jo, oba*, how are you?" he said. "Sorry I'm late."

He reached for a can of Orange Crush from the cooler and raised his index finger at the server. She added it to his tab. There was a tray of *plautz* in the cooler as well, each piece individually wrapped in plastic, which he scanned very skeptically before saying "*jauma*" loud enough for the serving staff to hear.

"Good idea," I said. "They're not so fresh."

He noted that City Sheila seemed to be enjoying hers, but then commented that she'd only lived in Edenfeld for two decades and probably hadn't yet developed a sophisticated enough palate for such things.

Mr. Harder motioned for me to sit down. He even put his hand on my shoulder briefly and I found the physical contact to be rather out of character. Again, he apologized for being late and said I could charge him for an extra half hour. He shook his head.

"What passes for *plautz* these days ..."

I cleared a place at the table, brushing aside my crumbs, and put *The Harder Book* in front of him. I was excited to hear what he thought about my new discoveries.

"This should be useful, shouldn't it?" I asked. "Found it at a garage sale. They wanted ten dollars, but I got it for half that. Can you believe it?"

He inched his chair forward, opened the book, and paged through it indifferently, glancing up at me from the top of his glasses. Then he pushed the book back into my hands without bothering to close it.

"I'm familiar with *The Harder Book*," he said, pausing for a moment in an unsuccessful attempt to open his Orange Crush. "Listen, Timothy, I think we need to make a few changes."

"To *The Harder Book*?"

It was a stupid question. *The Harder Book* was already in print and had been for decades. It was hardcover. It was on the shelves of every Harder family in town. There simply was no changing *The Harder Book*.

"I don't think you quite understand me," he said.

I sure didn't. I closed the book. Perhaps he'd be interested in the article I found about his uncle who'd been in the *Selbstschutz* back in Russia. I had the page ready to go and marked with an insert from the church bulletin. Before I could show it to him, though, he reached out to stop me. His hand was cold. Mine was a little damp.

"Listen, Timothy ... I hate to tell you this, but ..."

At this point, the server checked in and, noticing that Mr. Harder had still not opened the can, offered to pour it into a glass for him.

"Need a straw?" she asked.

"No, I won't be staying long," he said. "I'll take it with me."

"Well, anyway," I said, "I was thinking about chapter four where David is standing before Judge Adamson and—"

"You're not hearing me," said Mr. Harder.

"Was it Judge Adamson or Judge Embury?"

He shook his head, slowly and with great difficulty, then rubbed his neck as if he wished he hadn't been quite so vigorous with the head-shaking.

"No, I mean you don't understand. We can't continue like this," he said. "The book you're writing for me."

I leaned back in my chair and motioned for more coffee. I thought maybe another cup would put this conversation back in a more productive direction. She arrived promptly and topped me up, but Mr. Harder covered his cup with his hand and stared at me.

"I'm sure you don't want to be bothered with this project anymore, do you?" he asked.

"What do you mean? Of course I do," I said, then clarified myself. "It's not a bother. I'm enjoying it."

He stood up, which took quite some effort, and turned his attention to the window. His wife was waiting in the car below, the seats packed full of watermelons.

"Well, Timothy, I wish we could continue, but we have to consider other factors," he said. "Today will be our last meeting, I'm afraid."

"Seriously? Why? I thought things were going well."

I couldn't figure it out. Had my Iron Maiden T-shirts finally set him off? Perhaps he'd found a more affordable option, a willing relative who could hunt-and-peck their way through a manuscript.

"What should I do differently?" I asked. "I'd be glad to hear about any changes you'd like me to make. Your feedback would be very useful."

Mr. Harder didn't answer, but handed me a cheque.

"I think this should cover the work you've done so far," he said, then rummaged around in his pocket for a five-dollar bill. "And this is for the Orange Crush … and the coffee."

I slipped the cheque into my wallet without looking at it. Mr. Harder took his unconsumed beverage and ambled over to the door where Ernie helped him down the stairs. I glanced out the window and saw his wife slide the watermelons over to make room for her husband. I waved as he left, but I'm not sure he noticed. By that time, the women in the floral dresses were gone too.

I waited for a while, finished my coffee, and paid the bill. I hadn't been able to give Mr. Harder the bucket of freshly picked weeds. As I made my way out of the building, I told City Sheila that she could take the table, and keep the dandelions too, if she wished.

# Two

After being let go by Mr. Harder, I didn't feel like going out anywhere for a while, let alone attending the next Preservation Society meeting. I figured there were other things I could do with my Tuesday evening besides sitting in a church basement drinking decaf while chatting about history with people twice my age. Katie said I needed to adjust my attitude. She pointed out that we hadn't missed a meeting all year and I'd already spent enough time licking my wounds. When I said we couldn't afford to bring the cookies, Katie pointed out that we weren't on baked goods duty for at least another month. She also reminded me that we'd be watching the classic 1978 documentary *A Plane People: The Story of Mennonite Aviation* and she knew I didn't want to miss that. She always has a way of reminding me of the things I like.

"Besides," Katie observed, "it's a lovely evening for a walk."

This comment, she clarified, referred only to the weather and was no indication of her more conflicted views about strolling down Edenfeld's Main Street.

"It's got more gaps than Reverend Broesky's theology," she noted as we wandered hand-in-hand past vacant lots filled with dust and garbage. A few stained mattresses and a tractor tire that had not yet made its way to one of the local playgrounds leaned against the side of the credit union building. Yes, there was still a credit union, a couple churches, a gas station, and a mostly vacant strip mall with a Chinese restaurant, but all these buildings were separated by gaping holes, like the whole town had picked a fight with that mean, hulking Kroeker boy from over there in Bergthal.

According to some, however, our horribly disfigured Main Street is all part of a grand and cunning plan. "Soon," the mayor regularly proclaims, "we'll have a space large enough to fit that megamart."

After a few blocks of dusty lots, we passed the yard of the famous Lepp homestead which, if I'm being precise, is more ashy than dusty after the midnight fire that brought down the historic housebarn about a year ago. Now all that remains is a burned-out carcass that awaits some great repurposing, and a singed plaque that reads:

EDENFELD HERITAGE SITE. EST. 1881.

The town had been using the Lepp housebarn to store herbicide and backhoes and the fact that all the town's equipment was at a job site a few blocks away on the night of the fire only fuelled local conspiracy theories. "It's like Pearl Harbor," Randall observed. "Most of the ships weren't even there when the Japanese attacked." He said he read all this online somewhere.

A temporary fence had been put up around the Lepp property, meant to keep gawkers and scavengers at bay. DANGER, CONSTRUCTION ZONE. Katie didn't want to stand there very long.

"It's depressing," she said, so we kept on walking.

We walked a few more blocks down Main. When we got to Rodeo Drive, I squeezed Katie's hand and stopped briefly in front of Koop Convenience on the corner.

"The Heppner housebarn used to be right here," I said. "Lived there the first twenty years of my life."

Katie already knew this, of course, but gripped my hand appreciatively like it was the very first time I was disclosing this information. She said she wished she had known me back then so she could have paid me a visit, but I said I didn't think she would have been too impressed with the adolescent version of myself.

"I've shown you my junior high photos, right?"

Katie laughed and said my bowl cut and oversized Chicago Bulls jersey were absolutely adorable.

The street was even called Heppner Strasse for decades before BLT came up with the "revolutionary idea" to ditch the German and remove all the pioneering family names that were "no longer relevant." According to our mayor, the community is much better served with street names lifted randomly from a map of southern California. For a while, Main Street was supposed to be renamed

Hollywood Boulevard, but everyone thought that might be going a bit too far.

The Heppner family housebarn was demolished, along with about seven others, in the early 2000s, an era that Mayor BLT affectionately calls The Great Leap Forward. After I left home and my brother moved to the northern Alberta oil sands, my parents sold the property, saying they wanted "a nice modern house with heated floors and air conditioning," which they found way out on the west coast where it rains ten months a year. Now, in its place, stands the Koop convenience store, which is mostly used to provide twenty-four-hour access to sunflower seeds, and another two empty rental spots, one of which was briefly home to a sushi bar—a fascinating place to watch inexperienced Edenfelders drench carefully made nigiri in soy sauce with their fingers. The moment the Heppner barn went down, though, I was sad that I hadn't done more to save it. Soon after that, I joined the Preservation Society.

We stood there for a while at Koop Convenience. A Holdeman family was selling corn from the back of a pickup truck and I promised Katie we'd stop and buy a few ears on our way home later. I could smell the distinct bouquet of the feed mill in the distance. Katie pulled me close, moved by the beauty of empty lots and the smell of pellet production, and kissed me on the cheek.

"It's like all the Heppners were raptured a decade ago," she said, looking down our very sleepy version of Rodeo Drive. "I'm sure glad you got left behind."

Then Mrs. Koop came out wielding a broom and scooted us off the property. "*Rüt met die!* No loitering!"

By the time we arrived at South Edenfeld Mennonite Church for the meeting, everyone else was there and already a few coffee cups in. We'd missed the Mennonite aviation movie altogether and Mr. Wiebe was eager to move along with the proceedings. He pulled up a couple chairs, handed us each a butter tart, and told us to take our seats around the table.

I sat between Mrs. Friesen and Mrs. Ens while Katie wedged herself between Mr. Wiebe and Brenda, the only other active member under fifty who, due to her position at the local credit union, is more commonly referred to by locals as "that Brenda from the loans department." She has an encyclopedic knowledge of Anabaptist heroes from centuries ago which is entrenched in her memory and plastered all over her body in the form of tattoos.

"Good," said Mr. Wiebe. "Looks like we've reached quorum."

I counted. There were six of us.

Mr. Wiebe stood up and pulled the cap off a thick black marker, the scent of which immediately had me feeling a bit woozy.

"I assume you've all brought your pamphlets with you," he said.

We had. Katie poked around in her purse, then reached across the table and handed it to me. *A Historic Walking Tour of Edenfeld*. It had a map and a description of all the heritage sites in the area. Mrs. Friesen put it together one summer in the 1980s before BLT was mayor, and it's been photocopied and re-photocopied to the point where it's almost completely illegible.

Mrs. Friesen glanced at my map and bemoaned the unappreciated hours of work she had put into it.

"Took me nearly a year to put it together," she said.

Mrs. Ens, who I think joined the Preservation Society primarily so she could showcase her baking talents and keep her friends in line, interjected that, as she recalled it, Mrs. Friesen had spent most of the summer of 1985 snatching up bargains from the basement at Eaton's.

Mrs. Friesen waved off her friend's comment and told me not to believe a word of it. "I'm afraid that Mrs. Ens has a tendency to exaggerate," she said, "especially about the bargains that were available in the 80s."

Mr. Wiebe called for our attention.

"Time for the annual revision," he said, holding up the pamphlet.

He unfolded it, revealing the map on the inside, and put a big black *X* through the Lepp barn, the Rempel store, and a few other places that had met their demise in the last year, and then held it up for us to follow his example. He passed around the marker.

"Please update your maps," he said, "if you haven't already done so."

Mr. Wiebe is a retired science teacher, but his real passion is local architecture. He spent many a summer working on a book about our building practices called *Longing for Housebarns: Blueprints and Poems*.

"The humble housebarn," Mr. Wiebe said, as we inhaled black marker fumes and updated our maps, "more than any other example of Mennonite architecture, represents our pragmatism, our work ethic, and our connection to the land. I can think of no more vital representation of our heritage."

He said these buildings were something we should be proud of, though there was some debate about whether we should be "proud" of our housebarns or simply "appreciative" until Katie said the difference was merely semantics and perhaps we were getting sidetracked.

"Regardless, we have to save the ones we have," said Mr. Wiebe.

"The *one* we have, you mean," Mrs. Friesen reminded him.

She was referring to the housebarn owned by Randall's parents. It's known as the Hiebert housebarn, after Randall's father, and is right next to the empty lot on Mulholland (formerly Klippenstein) Drive, where they hold farm equipment auctions in the spring and build a skating rink every winter, complete with a shack where you can warm up with hot chocolate or get your skates sharpened for a nominal fee. "The property hasn't yet reached its potential," BLT often says while casting a side-eye at the Hiebert barn. In Edenfeld, there's nothing more dangerous to your health than to sit in close proximity to an empty lot.

Despite the fact that we both grew up in preservation-worthy buildings, I haven't been able to get Randall to come to these meetings. He says he prefers to spend his Tuesday nights making home-brewed beer in his garage and scouring the Internet for eligible life partners. I tried to convince him that he might find a woman at the Preservation Society meetings, but he reminded me that I usually refer to the group members as my "grandparents."

Mr. Wiebe said the plaque outside the Hiebert

housebarn could use an update. Maybe it could be modified to include some information about its original owners, the Klippensteins. He said he was willing to write the text if Katie and I would give it a proofread, a task which everyone affirmed by show of hands. None of us wanted to repeat the fiasco they recently had over in Neu-Kronsberg where they spent two thousand dollars on a huge commemorative cairn honouring the town's pioneers, only to find it had been autocorrected to "Nude-Kronsberg," an error that disappointed dozens of frat boys who drove in from the city one weekend to find nothing but a dull prairie town and its fully clothed inhabitants.

There are dozens of these plaques all over town, installed during Edenfeld's centennial celebrations in 1976. There is one in front of each of our five churches, some businesses, a couple trees, a few private residences, and even next to a "heritage boot scraper" out on La Brea that contains the petrified boot-scrapings of early Edenfeld pioneer and world-famous cheesemaker Johann B. Peters. That's what the sign says anyway. This was all long before BLT became mayor. Not a single plaque has been put up since.

Mr. Wiebe also mentioned that someone should go over to the Lepp barn and at least straighten out the signage because the Parks and Rec crew had accidentally backed over it when they were cleaning up the property. He looked at me.

"I'm afraid I can't," I said. "BLT banned it."

"He banned sign-straightening?" said Brenda from Loans.

"Well, not in those exact words, but the Lepp barn is

on civic property and Mr. Vogt says it's a waste of taxpayer dollars and that the money could be much better spent on snow clearing and when I pointed out that it was still summer, he said I wasn't thinking ahead, which was 'typical for my generation.'"

I'm amazed that the Preservation Society members tolerate me as much as they do. Thankfully, they don't judge me for the fact that I'm one of BLT's "henchmen" on the Parks and Rec department, though whenever the name is recorded in the minutes, Mrs. Friesen always writes "Parks and Wreck." They understand that there aren't any other viable employment options in Edenfeld for a man my age who's not so great with livestock. I think they also decided that having an "insider" on the committee might be of use someday.

"Oh, don't be ridiculous," Katie said. "Just go over there and do it. I'll do it myself if you won't. We also might as well straighten out the Hiebert sign while we're at it. It looks like an accidental victim of the Thiessen boys too."

"I'll go with her," said Brenda from Loans.

She turned in her seat and stood up as if to go right then, and when she did, we all got a clear view of a tattoo on the small of her back. It was the image of a man, though her skin was so thoroughly spray-tanned that it made his precise identity difficult to determine.

Mrs. Friesen bit into a butter tart and, speaking with a couple raisins clinging to her upper lip, piped up, "Is that new, Brenda?"

"Yeah. Got to cover it up at work, though," she said. "They're not too keen on tattoos. They say it's unprofessional."

She hiked up her shirt a few inches and spun around for us all to see. Mrs. Friesen raised her eyebrows. Mrs. Ens looked down at her plate of cookies. Mr. Wiebe immediately excused himself to the bathroom. Brenda from Loans looked right at Katie, who smiled cautiously, then over at me. She wanted us to guess.

I picked legendary church elder Klaas Reimer. Katie said John Holdeman. Mrs. Friesen thought that it was Conrad Grebel.

"*Na*, I don't know about that," Mrs. Ens said, but offered no guess of her own.

We were all wrong.

"It's Johann Cornies," Brenda from Loans proclaimed. "The nineteenth-century agricultural reformer!"

I complimented the tattoo, just to be nice, although secretly I doubted Mr. Cornies's sideburns were as bushy as the artist made them out to be.

"That's remarkable, Brenda," said Mrs. Friesen. "It really shows your commitment to the values of the Preservation Society."

"I've got a few martyrs too," Brenda from Loans continued. "Real heroes who died for their faith, so I can be reminded of them all the time. You know what I mean? You should see the one I've got of Dirk Willems crossing the icy river ..."

We told her we'd examine Dirk Willems another day.

"You know who my favourite martyr is?" Katie said. "Elsie Dyck. It's really too bad what happened to her. Being run out of town like that. I really don't think she poisoned all those people."

Mrs. Friesen agreed that she didn't believe that story,

but everyone else said there was no other plausible explanation for why Edenfeld's most celebrated writer had left
town twenty-five years ago and never returned.

You've heard of Elsie Dyck, I'm sure. Her third novel,
*Scandalous Quotations from a Mennonite Diary*, was
released to rave reviews in the mid-nineties. For a lot of
Edenfelders, she was a real source of pride. "Our Elsie"
had made it big. Not everyone was a fan, however. Some
powerful folks around here were pretty quick to denounce
her, pointing out that she hadn't been to church in years
and it had been even longer since she'd touched an udder.
Despite all the accolades she garnered from the outside
world, the only recognition Elsie Dyck ever received in
Edenfeld was a brief blurb buried deep in the local paper.
"Former Edenfelder Releases New Book. Don't Read It.
You'll Regret It. Trust Me." Something like that. As far as
I know, the book was never sold here in town. Katie and I
do have a copy, but then, we drive into the city every once
in a while to purchase forbidden items like Elsie Dyck
novels and PG-13 movies.

I've wanted to be a writer ever since I first read Elsie's
books as a teenager. The fact that her books were unofficially banned in town and I had to hide them under my
pillow at night was at least part of the appeal. Beyond
that, though, her writing was brilliant and truthful in
a way I'd never experienced before. She didn't ideal-
ize our past, but she wrote about Edenfeld, which she
cleverly renamed Gardenfield, as a place of nuance,
where behind the headscarves and manure-encrusted
rubber boots were real people with desires and passions for slightly nicer headscarves and slightly less

manure-encrusted boots. These were modest desires, sure, but they were desires nonetheless. BLT despises her books. He says we need not dwell on the past or stir up "unnecessary passions," for that matter. We certainly don't need to be putting our regrettable history on display for the whole world to see. "Her book is an embarrassment," he said at one of his modestly attended council meetings. "It's not conducive to economic growth. Simply put, Elsie Dyck is bad for business."

I explained all this to the others, revealing my "unnecessary passion" for the work of Elsie Dyck, but by then Mr. Wiebe had returned and said it probably wasn't such a wise idea to go around proclaiming my undying love for Edenfeld's most recent martyr. He feared for the safety of my fingers.

"BLT's a powerful man."

Mrs. Friesen said that was nonsense and that no finger-breaking had ever occurred to her knowledge.

Mrs. Ens shook her head and displayed her fingers, which did look a little crooked, but Mrs. Friesen attributed her friend's slight disfigurement to rheumatism and excessive quilting and told Mrs. Ens to stop fearmongering.

"He may not have broken her fingers," Mrs. Ens admitted, "but remember that artisanal bakery she ran to supplement her writing income? I heard that BLT was so upset over her writing that he had her shut down and fined by the health inspector, who happened to be his nephew. All on account of some supposedly undercooked cookie dough. They claimed eleven people were hospitalized after a church luncheon."

"And she wasn't allowed inside a church after that, either," added Mr. Wiebe.

"That's probably just as well," said Katie.

"It's hard to make it as an Edenfeld writer in the best of times," continued Mrs. Ens, "let alone when you can't sell sugar cookies on the side or broker business deals in the church lobby. She might have even faced prison time for making all those people sick, but BLT agreed to drop all charges and destroy the evidence so long as she agreed to leave town forever and cease writing about it. Of course, I heard all this from Mrs. Barkman, and you know how reliable she is, but anyway, that's the story."

Mrs. Friesen reminded us that stories in Edenfeld were often embellished with great success and rapidity, and that those coming from Mrs. Barkman were especially suspect. She said not to worry, that Elsie Dyck was living in the city and doing just fine. She claimed it wasn't so long ago, actually, that she'd seen her at the Snow View Mall food court cheerfully hoisting an A&W root beer. She said she'd shared an order of onion rings with her more than a few times.

I had serious doubts about Mrs. Friesen's supposed Elsie Dyck sightings and was about to express them, but Katie looked at me and kicked me under the table, which was always the signal that perhaps I should keep my mouth shut.

"You all know that 553 Melrose is going up for sale, right?" said Mrs. Friesen.

The Preservation Society has been trying to get a plaque at 553 Melrose for years but there's always been strong resistance. Nobody thinks that Elsie Dyck's childhood home is worthy of a plaque and the people who live there now don't want all the extra attention it would draw. They might have to mow the lawn more often or put on a shirt before peering out the living room window. The house might even be photographed by city people on occasion. All of this is considered a great nuisance. "Besides," they argue, "is this Elsie Dyck really so important anyway?"

At this point, Mr. Wiebe indicated that neither Elsie Dyck nor the Elsie Dyck house were on the agenda for the evening, after which Katie shot up her hand and made a motion to have these topics added so that we could continue our discussion.

"All in favour, say 'aye.'"

We all said "aye," although Mrs. Ens shouted "*oba jo*" and Mr. Wiebe made her re-vote in English to make it official, even though we already had more than enough ayes without her *oba jo* to carry the motion.

After further discussion, we concluded that we'd probably never have the funds to purchase 553 Melrose and turn it into a museum like they did in Neepawa once the locals decided they actually liked Margaret Laurence, but we figured at the very least the new owners might be receptive to a historic marker. As far as we knew, the building, and all the houses around it, were owned by some out-of-town investment company, but Mrs. Ens said she'd talk to her daughter, a realtor, and see if she could sell it to people who were "well-informed of the house's historic and literary significance." Not that she expected her to in any way jeopardize her potential commission. "But maybe it would be a selling point," she said, "if people were aware that Elsie Dyck once lived there."

Brenda from Loans said she'd talk to the credit union to see if they'd be willing to sponsor the project. "Even if they don't give us the money outright, at the very least I think I can score us an affordable interest rate."

We were all very grateful to have someone like Brenda from Loans on the committee.

"It's nice to see some young people taking an interest in our history," said Mr. Wiebe.

Katie, Brenda, and I were all approaching forty, and none of us thought of ourselves as particularly young any-more, but we had no other way of interpreting this com-ment than to assume it was directed at us.

"Thanks," said Katie. "I wish there were others."

"Me too," Mr. Wiebe said. "Especially around the may-oral election." He reminded us of BLT's slogan from the most recent election: *Values of the Past. Strip Malls of the Future.*

"That was on all his signs," he said.

"Those signs were always straight," I noted.

"Oh, don't worry," Katie said. "We'll get the Lepp sign looking great."

I wasn't worried as much about the plaque as I was about maintaining my job at the Parks and Rec depart-ment. I told them I'd try to be involved in other ways, but was deliberately vague on the details.

Mrs. Friesen said the Preservation Society had gone long enough without a slogan of our own, and if BLT was going to have one, then so should we.

"Buildings of the Past. Values of the Future," she suggested.

Mr. Wiebe said the slogan was a bit derivative, possibly

alienating, and that we should stick to preserving buildings and need not say anything about progressive values. Mrs. Ens agreed, though when we put it to a vote, she sided with Mrs. Friesen and the motion to adopt the new slogan passed by a count of five to one and even Mr. Wiebe, who was the lone vote against the motion, said he was okay with it and would continue to attend the meetings.

"We'll start by straightening signs," Katie said, "and go from there."

"In the dead of night, I hope," warned Mr. Wiebe.

Katie nodded.

"Well, I think we've made some real progress here," said Mrs. Ens.

I wasn't entirely sure whether she was referring to the signs, the Elsie Dyck house, or the fact that Mrs. Friesen had finally baked some butter tarts that met her standards.

# Three

The first time I saw Katie I was sitting on a wooden pew in wet swimming trunks as she was coming up out of the water. It was a singles event at South Edenfeld. I call it a "singles" event because that's how all the young people viewed it, though officially it was a baptismal class. The class was specifically designed for "late bloomers" like us who hadn't done it like you're supposed to during the summer between your high school graduation and your wedding day. Katie and I, however, were well into our twenties by then, so we got put in a class with the other heathens and people who'd recently moved into town from the city. It's not that I didn't believe or didn't want to get baptized as a teenager, but in those days I hadn't yet found someone I wanted to marry and I knew that as soon as I was baptized the pressure would be on to get hitched to the nearest and most convenient young woman in brown nylons named Edna.

Before they let you get baptized, they make you take classes where you learn about martyrs and the Sermon on the Mount and the true meaning of the ritual and why our particular baptismal method, at our particular church, is superior to the others. To longtime Edenfelders, this is old news, but to people like City Sheila, who was also in our class, there was quite the learning curve. There are so many nuances. We have a handful of Mennonite churches in town, but they agree on almost nothing, except that the Lutherans have got it all wrong with the whole baptizing babies thing. Right before your teenage wedding is much better.

Unlike most of the churches around here, though, we're dunkers. We believe a baptism doesn't actually count unless you're soaking and shivering, clothes clinging to your body when you're finished. We get a lot of heat for this from the other churches who prefer to fill a plastic cup with tap water and slowly, solemnly, pour it on the candidate's head.

That day, I was sitting there in the sanctuary next to the baptismal tank, waiting for my turn. I'd hit my head in my first practice dunk because I hadn't bent my knees the way I was supposed to and Reverend Broesky said I could have another go at it once the others had a chance.

Katie walked in ten minutes after seven o'clock, her chin up, confident, and Reverend Broesky said that since she had the audacity to show up late for practice, she must be "well versed in the matter and may as well show the others how it's done."

She went in and out like a synchronized swimmer and when she was finished the reverend handed her a towel and commended her on her form and stamina, but suggested she should work on her backstroke.

Katie smiled at me on her way out, while I rubbed the back of my head and made a feeble attempt to return the gesture.

"On Sunday, wear comfortable, loose-fitting clothes," Reverend Broesky said. "And absolutely no white!"

Like so many rules, Katie disregarded this one completely. When Sunday came, she wore ripped denim jeans and a blazing white Sonic Youth T-shirt. We started dating almost immediately after, before our clothes had even dried, which just confirmed everything the pourers thought about the evils of dunking and even had some of the dunkers questioning their own doctrine too. Apparently, matchmaking was to be reserved for *faspa* and martyr class, and we were told that our minds were to be kept pure and we weren't actually "supposed to be thinking about such things while the baptisms are taking place."

Katie is from Altfeld, a village about thirty kilometres down a gravel road from Edenfeld, which is why we didn't meet until we were both old and haggard. You'd think that around here, everyone would know everyone else, but that's not the case. If you go to South Edenfeld Church, you have very little contact with the Lutherans or EMMCers or MBers or KGers or the folks over at the Faith Barn. In fact, other than fighting over the last remaining chicken ball at the Chinese buffet after the Sunday morning service, there's little reason for us to interact. It also didn't help that Randall and I went to Edenfeld's private Mennonite school and Katie bussed over to the public school in Ste. Adèle where they had an arts program and a rugby team. At our school, we only had flannelgraph boards and contact-free sports like crokinole and horseshoes. Katie moved to Edenfeld when she was a teenager because her father got a job selling teat dip to dairy farmers, but even then we didn't cross paths because her family went to the wrong church. Thankfully, the Great Schism of 2006 brought fifty or sixty disgruntled Faith Barners across town to our con-gregation. I think the split was over whether to use real wine or Welch's grape juice during communion. Whatever the reason, the Brandt family eventually found themselves at South Edenfeld and even though Katie had already been baptized in Altfeld as a teenager, she had to get it done all over again properly at our church.

Before Katie and I met, everyone thought I'd never get married since I was in my late twenties and still single. Katie was in an even worse position because, at twen-ty-five, she was considered an old maid and her unmar-ried aunts had already asked her to come live with them; it was either that or become a missionary. They didn't understand the university thing either. "It's like a Bible school without the Bible," Katie tried to explain, but they couldn't see what the point of that would be. I'd like to think that Katie waited so long to get married because she had high standards and didn't want to marry the farmer her mom had picked out for her, but more likely it was because she was an ambitious student and wanted to finish her bachelor's degree first. Then, one summer, we proved all the naysayers wrong. We had a quick two-hour ceremony and a reception in the church basement. It was a typical Edenfeld wedding with no dancing and no alcohol but plenty of whipped-cream-based salads.

I'd finally decided to get baptized because I thought it was time to settle down, and also because Randall said it might help attract ghostwriting clients. "No one wants to have their book written by an unbaptized pagan," he'd said.

Just as Randall predicted, I saw a significant uptick in business after my baptism, and even more once Katie and I got married. Edenfelders love to know their money is going to support a righteous cause such as a good, wholesome marriage like ours. Lately, though, the effect of the baptism seems to have worn off.

A couple weeks after Mr. Harder sent me packing, I lost Mr. Loewen. He had me working on a rather ambitious book called *Lions Without Teeth: The Story of the Loewen Family from 1540 to the Present Day*. I was somewhere in the late 1700s when he called the whole thing off. He broke the news to me in the picnic shelter at BLT Wiens Memorial Park, while we snacked on cold pieces of raw farmer sausage that his wife had sent along with strict instructions to dip them in white vinegar before consuming. He fired me without explanation, claiming he was following the biblical model found in the Gospel of Matthew: "If thy brother shall trespass against thee, go and tell him his fault." And ply him with *foarmaworscht*, apparently.

Since he was unable to articulate how I had trespassed against him, I probably could have sued for breach of contract or something, but it isn't our way to sue. We're supposed to resolve issues amongst ourselves without involving the outside world. I think that rule was put in place in about 1987 when a younger BLT Wiens stopped

Mr. Kliewer from building Edenfeld's first high-rise apartment block, only to close down two flour mills employing dozens of people to build one himself a few years later. Mr. Kliewer threatened legal action, but everyone in town told him to calm right down and let the church elders settle things, which they did by voting overwhelmingly in favour of Mr. Wiens, who happened to be the bigger tither.

Like Mr. Harder, Mr. Loewen didn't give me a good reason for my removal. Vinegar dripping from his fingers, he claimed I'd missed a few evening services and said he'd finish the book on his own or get help from his granddaughter Melissa. "She's a blogger," he said.

I couldn't figure out what was going on. I'd been ghostwriting for years and had never lost a client before, not right in the middle of a project, anyway, and never because they were dissatisfied with my services. Then, out of nowhere, I lost two clients in quick succession. I don't want to confirm any stereotypes about the frugality of Mennonites, but when I lost a second customer, the first thing I thought about was the state of our finances. Katie had gone back to do her master's on the assumption I'd be able to pay the mortgage all on my own, which rested on the assumption I'd have a few ghostwriting jobs alongside my Parks and Rec salary, which rested on the assumption that my adult baptism and my ability to start a new Word document would guarantee more ghostwriting business than I could ever want. Now, all that was falling apart. Perhaps another dunking was in order.

After my encounter with Mr. Loewen in the picnic shelter, Katie and I went over to Randall's bungalow on Crenshaw Boulevard to discuss what was happening to my ghostwriting business. Rather, we went over to the single-car garage attached to Randall's bungalow, which is where the three of us have been congregating ever since we started Edenfeld's first rock band about ten years ago. We like to say we were the first, anyway, but Mrs. Ens says that there were plenty of "rebel Mennonites" in town long before we came around. She claims that in 1975 she became the first woman ever to sit in the men's section at South Edenfeld Mennonite Church. She squeezed in right next to Elder Voth's son Darren. She even grabbed a corner of his hymnal. "Things never worked out between me and him," she said, "but soon everyone at South Edenfeld sat wherever they pleased. It took someone to be the first." Mrs. Friesen denies this story, but it seems to hold up to examination. Just after Mrs. Ens's infamous hymnal grab, South Edenfeld became known as the most progressive church in town and remained so until West Edenfeld Church changed its name to the Faith Barn, hired a youth pastor with a goatee, and spruced up the old hymns with a pedal steel guitar. That's a problem in Edenfeld, it seems; everyone has conflicting concepts of progress.

Anyway, our rock band lasted for a couple years, until we realized our Bruce Springsteen covers weren't all that good and that we weren't going to sign a major record deal while playing in Randall's garage. We keep hanging out there, though. It's a habit. It's also where Randall has his homebrewing equipment, which might explode, he says, if he doesn't tend to it all the time. However, I think the whole garage thing might have more to do with the fact that it reminds him of the housebarns we grew up in as children. When Katie made this comparison, though, Randall became defensive, saying his home was nothing like a barn. "I'm actually quite averse to animal possession," he said. "You know that, Katie."

Katie brought her laptop along. She's writing a thesis on gender performativity in traditional Mennonite households and didn't want to pass up the opportunity to complete a few more paragraphs. She's been working on it for a few years and has quite a lot to say.

"If the two of you start rambling on and on about brewer's yeast or something," she said, "at least I'll be able to get some work done."

When we arrived, we noticed some changes. For one thing, Randall's Audi was parked out on the street behind a row of minivans and pickup trucks. He needed the space to increase the brewing capacity of his garage. He pointed out the bags of barley and hops lining the wall and said he was considering making something called a Russian Imperial Stout. I tried to ask him about Mr. Harder and Mr. Loewen, but all he wanted to do was enlighten me on the wide world of hops and how some are for aroma and some are for taste and some contribute to the mouthfeel of a beer. He handed Katie a glass of thick, black liquid that made her recoil as soon as it touched her lips.

"Is this legal?" she asked, handing me the glass.

"Of course it is," Randall said, peering down the street in all directions before lowering the garage door completely.

Katie sat down on a bar stool, still there from her days as rhythm guitarist, and began filing her nails. She keeps them short. "I have to be able to type," she says. I looked for a place to sit but found nothing, so Randall slid over a couple bags of malt and told me to "sit my butt down for once." Katie again joked about the place being like a house-barn and this time Randall couldn't deny the similarities.

"So, about your ghostwriting problem," Randall said, now ready to discuss matters of importance. "It seems to me the issue is all marketing. I mean, what's your brand? You know, the Heppner brand? You've gotta do a lot more than just leave a few business cards with the roofing guys at Kehler Hardware."

"Kehler Hardware?" I said. "That's a great idea."

"My point is," Randall continued, "I really don't think you're getting your name out there. Your methods are far too traditional."

He always tells me that, but I maintain that Randall's not quite the anti-traditionalist he claims to be. He even allows a few words of Plautdietsch to slip through once in a while. Every time it happens, he apologizes, as if speaking the mother tongue of our people is something to be ashamed of. I certainly don't think it is. In fact, I'm ashamed I don't know it better. Katie and I even tried to learn for a while, but all I can say is "*Schinda em Schiet!*" and "*Waut de schissjat!*" and both phrases could get me excommunicated if I ever said them anywhere other than in the stands of a hockey rink. We never had the chance to learn more; the mayor's been crusading against Plautdietsch for decades. He thinks our language is "unrefined" and encourages parents to stick a bar of soap in their children's mouths anytime they speak it. Thanks to his efforts, the language is dying off like the elm trees and Sunday evening church singalongs.

I told Randall I didn't think marketing was the issue. People know my name; it's right there in the ad on the bulletin board at the post office. It says:

GHOSTWRITING AND EDITING SERVACES
*Family history books! Genealogies! Historical fiction!*
REASONIBLE RATES
*Contact: Timothy B. Heppner, Edenfeld, Manitoba*

Randall has never ceased to ridicule me about the typos. Below the ad are long, thin strips of paper with my phone number. I removed a few, so it looked like I was in high demand, and every once in a while I go over to check on it to make sure it hasn't been covered up with postings for one of Mrs. Guenther's bi-weekly garage sales or business cards for Mr. Wall's dubious chiropractic services.

"I think I'm doing okay in the marketing department," I said.

Randall poured himself another glass of homebrew. Somehow he'd already drained two glasses while I had barely touched my first. I was about to snap a photo, you know, to document our good times for social media, but Randall pushed his beer out of view. He said he couldn't risk having such a photo show up online somewhere.

"I don't need that kind of reputation," Randall said.

I put my phone away.

"See, this is your problem, Timothy," he said. "You've got to be more careful with your image. Somehow your Heppner brand's been tainted."

"Dude, you wrote a sex book and still have plenty of business."

I'm not sure if you're aware of this, but the primary

reason Randall's been able to ghostwrite full-time is thanks to the revenue he's got streaming in from the couple books he wrote with his own name on them. He's no Elsie Dyck, mind you, but his books have done fairly well around here, at least among South Edenfeld members and Lutherans. You may have heard of them. One is called *The Pale Mennonite* and the other is *Everything You Wanted to Know About Mennonite Sex *But Were Afraid to Ask*.

Katie looked up from her computer.

"Yeah, why hasn't BLT run you out of town?" she asked.

"Why would he?"

"Well, Elsie Dyck didn't have such a good time of it," she said. "It's odd. Why haven't you suffered any loss of business?"

"Loss of hair, perhaps," I noted, and it was not untrue.

The first time I met Randall, he had a big mop of curly hair that obstructed my view of Mary Epp on the bus ride over to the old folks' home. It was his first day attending Edenfeld Mennonite School, one of those quirky schools where we basically worked on our own in little cubicles and raised a blue flag when we needed assistance or a red flag when we really needed to pee. Our teachers, who were just older high school students, or people who had graduated the year before, made us watch a lot of VHS tapes about missionaries and once a month we took a bus to Golden Slumbers Retirement Manor where we sang "Praise God From Whom All Blessings Flow" and read them a few Bible verses, and this was where Randall got in my sight-line, blocking any chance I had at a romantic school bus encounter with Mary Epp. Thanks to him, I never did get to hold her hand across the aisle. I was probably the only boy in the class who didn't. Well, Randall didn't either. Years later, still clinging to his principles, he told me, "I'm saving hand-holding for marriage."

Randall stood, a little unsteady on his feet, and reached to the top shelf above his brewing equipment. Between two half-depleted containers of windshield washer fluid, he found a book that he tossed onto Katie's lap.

"You want to know why I'm doing all right?" Randall said. "The difference between me and Elsie Dyck? The difference between me and Timothy? Well, Timothy and Elsie never wrote *A Man of Vision: The BLT Wiens Story.*"

This particular book documents BLT's life, from his humble beginnings as a lowly farmhand to his establishment of a highly automated quilt factory that put all the grannies out of business. The book was recently added to the local school curriculum. The kids love it. *BLT Wiens II: The Phantom Menno* was planned but never got published, which was very disappointing to die-hard fans who were hoping for a sequel.

"The worst thing you ever wrote," Katie said.

She pinched the edge of the book, not really wanting to touch it, and passed it off to me.

"Hey, it's not that bad," Randall said. "You probably haven't even read it."

Katie acknowledged the truth of that statement, but said she had no interest in remedying the situation.

I handed the book back to Randall.

"I also seconded for him a few times," Randall said.

"You seconded?"

"Yeah, at the Edenfeld Progress Committee meetings."

The Edenfeld Progress Committee is another one of BLT's initiatives. Basically, he wants it to look like he has public approval for all his demolitions, so he set up an advisory panel of hand-picked and supposedly representative members of the community to "weigh in on critical issues."

"Weren't you invited?" Randall asked.

Katie scoffed and mentioned something she'd read in one of her classes. Noam Chomsky. *Manufacturing Consent.* It went over our heads.

"Anyway, it's all arranged ahead of time," Randall explained. "He raises a motion, looks in my general direction, and I second it. Simple. Otherwise it takes forever and there's a lengthy discussion and, you know how Edenfelders are, things go nowhere. But if you can get that seconder really quick, then it's all a lot smoother."

"What sort of things did you second?" I asked.

"I don't know. I don't really pay attention."

"The elms by the Co-op? The Lepp barn?"

"Look, I have no idea what I seconded," he said. "Most of the time I'm texting or listening to Pearl Jam. All I know is when BLT gives me the look, I raise my hand and the woman at the laptop says, 'Motion seconded by Randall Hiebert.' I don't have time for all the details."

"Or how about BLT's five-point manifesto? Did you second that?"

It was printed in last week's newspaper, a full-page ad on the front of the Faith section, which is always the most-read section of *The Edenfeld Rubbernecker.* Randall claimed not to be aware of it, but he gave himself away when he glanced at the stack of old newspapers in the recycling bin. There on the top was the most recent issue, which had beer stains all over it and exhibited all the signs of having been thoroughly examined.

Katie opened it to the Faith section and started reading out loud.

"Seeing as a big-box store is of upmost importance for the long-term economic, social, and spiritual well-being of the Town of Edenfeld, we, the undersigned, urge the council to enact, and the community to support, the following initiatives:

"Number one: Clearing the town of any unoccupied or otherwise unusable buildings at the earliest convenience, and eliminating all barriers to progress that may seek to maintain these buildings for purposes that do not fit this goal.

"Number two: Establishing a marketing campaign to promote our community, attract new families, and create a positive and growing atmosphere.

"Number three: Upholding the values that sustained and maintained Edenfeld during the tenure of Mayor Wiens: Family, Faith, and Fiscal Responsibility.

"Number four: Given the limited resources at our disposal, prioritizing those public works projects that would directly lead to creating an attractive market for outside investment.

"Number five: No straightening of historic markers or signs—"

"That's not what it says," Randall interrupted, grabbing the paper from Katie's hands.

"How would you know? I thought you didn't pay attention when you seconded things," Katie said. "No wonder you don't feel comfortable at the Preservation Society."

"It doesn't say anything about not straightening signs," he said.

"Well, not in those words," Katie said, "but if you're so confident BLT wouldn't have a problem with it, then why don't you join us?"

Randall stood up to check on the wort he was boiling and threw in what I observed to be an overly generous quantity of hops. He turned back around to speak.

"Look, the point is, if you want to make it as a ghost-writer, you've got to do more than what you're doing."

"You said it was going to be easy money," I recalled. "'Hey, you're a writer, Timothy. Want to earn some extra cash?'"

"That was years ago. Times have changed."

I remember when Randall first pitched the ghostwriting idea to me. Vague propositions of cash always made me nervous, but Randall said Mr. Petkau had paid him almost two thousand dollars. He said ghostwriting was a decent job if you could break into the racket and stay there. That's the key. Staying in the game. It's a never-ending cycle of Mr. Toews selling his self-published, long-winded religious testimony to Mr. Penner, who in turn sells Mr. Toews his account of his great-great-grandfather's time in Danzig. It's like a Ponzi scheme.

When I first started, I wasn't all that confident in my writing skills, but Randall said I was plenty good enough, even though my entire publication record consisted of one very ill-advised childhood political treatise and four editorials printed next to the Moonlight Girl in one of the city tabloids.

"You don't have to be great," he said. "You can start with Mrs. Fehr."

Esther Fehr wasn't the easiest client to work with, though, especially since I was new to this and she thought of herself as a real novelist. In our first meeting, she hauled out these notes about plot development and story structure from the creative writing course she once took at the Edenfeld Community Centre. "I've heard something about climaxes," Esther told me. I've been doing Randall's cast-offs ever since.

"If you want to continue as a ghostwriter in this town," Randall said, "you're going to have to attract some new clients ... either that, or move to the city."

Here in Edenfeld, the odds are against us. Randall says a town of our size can only have one famous writer in a century and there was already Elsie Dyck. He'd even printed off a pie chart that showed precisely the minimal odds we have of ever achieving anything worthwhile if we stay here. My sliver of hope was so thin, according to his chart, that even his cousin Benny had a better chance of making it on Broadway than I did of accomplishing anything of worth here in Edenfeld.

"Maybe it's time to give up ghostwriting," Randall said.

He told us he was thinking of leaving town, but then, he was always talking about that. I doubted he'd ever actually do it. It's hard to leave when you have your pick of all the top ghostwriting clients, and now some of mine, no doubt. He claimed he had plans, though. Imminent ones. You know, like the same imminent ones he'd had for the past fifteen years. He was always just about to make the big move to Moscow or London or, at the very least, Abbotsford, which I told him was the biggest Mennonite cliché I could imagine.

"Moving to the city is so twentieth century," I told him. "Who would I be in the city? Just another hayseed from the country trying to seek fame and fortune on Henderson Highway."

I figured it was about time all the "rebel Mennonites" stayed in their small towns, drank their craft beer, played in their Springsteen cover bands, and wrote their trashy novels.

Besides, I enjoy the work—the ghostwriting, I mean. Yes, some of the stories are on the repetitive side, and yes, some of my clients insist that I pick them up for our meetings and then, before turning down Sunset Strip, say, "We might as well stop by at Frugal Frank's for some fresh dillweed," but the work grounds me, gives me the sense that, despite everything I'm destroying during my day job, perhaps, in some way, I'm helping to restore it in the evenings.

"If we need the money, I could see if the gas station is hiring," said Katie.

I assumed she'd had a touch too much of Randall's home-brewed ale and told her so.

"No, really," she said. "If I have to take on a few shifts, I'll do it."

I wanted to tell her no, that wasn't necessary and it never would be, but the truth was, things were pretty tight and unless I picked up a few more clients, it might come to that.

"Never mind," Randall said. "It's all about marketing."

I wasn't so sure. Still, I had to do something. Who knows? Maybe my public image did require a revamp. I certainly didn't want to end up banished to the Snow View Mall food court like Elsie Dyck. I wasn't sure I could handle that volume of onion rings.

# Four

The sign-straightening took place a few days later. We would have done it sooner, but we had to wait until we could find an evening that fit Randall's busy schedule. He was not a member of the Preservation Society, but everyone thought I had neither the heft, nor the girth, to adjust the signs myself. Randall agreed to come along so long as we did it after eleven when everyone was asleep, except for the young men who drive up and down Sunset Strip all night in Honda Civics for no apparent reason. We could hear the squealing tires and smell the burning rubber three blocks away.

Katie said she'd stand guard at the end of the driveway while Randall and I heaved our bodies at the commemorative sign in front of the burned-out Lepp barn. Brenda from Loans stood nearby smoking a cigarette until Katie told her that we were trying to be inconspicuous and she quickly put it out. Randall began swatting at imaginary mosquitos and said we should hurry up and get it over with. I was good with that.

"One or two thrusts should do it," he said.

Brenda from Loans laughed.

"Aren't you supposed to be on the lookout?" Randall asked.

She said she'd do her very best to keep us safe and undetected and wandered over to join Katie, but I was concerned that Brenda from Loans wasn't taking her job all that seriously. Nor did I appreciate the fact that Katie had a camera hanging around her neck. I could think of no reason that any of this activity needed to be documented for posterity.

"I really shouldn't be doing this," I reminded Randall. "This is town-owned property."

"Wow, you're paranoid. Chill, Timothy."

I found this comment a bit strange coming from a man who doesn't want to be photographed with a beer glass. Randall's always worried about being watched. He even believes what they told us in Sunday school about how our dead relatives are watching us from above when we sin. I wonder what kind of an afterlife that would be. An eternity spent watching your grandchildren page longingly through your stash of old Eaton's catalogues? Katie, who voraciously read the *Anne of Green Gables* books as a child, says she was always worried she was being watched by Lucy Maud Montgomery.

Anyway, Randall telling me to "chill" was basically unprecedented and I wondered if Brenda's presence might have had something to do with it.

"Dude, shush," I said.

Randall looked over at Brenda, then loudly proclaimed that there was nothing to worry about and we wouldn't get caught and it was not such a big deal even if we did, but I reminded him of the fact that I was the only one of us who was risking their livelihood to preserve a bit of heritage.

"Parks and Rec is beneath you anyway," Randall said.

"I've got a mortgage to pay," I whispered. "I lost another client this week. Mr. Elias, head-coach-slash-evangelist of the Edenfeld Deacons softball team."

"Another one? I warned you, didn't I? Marketing …"

"It was a good project too," I said. "*A Sermon from the Dugout: The Bernie Elias Story.* You'd never believe how many relief pitchers he converted over the years. I really don't know what's happening. I can't quit my day job, that's for sure."

I stared at the housebarn, or what was left of it. What was the point of a sign when the building itself was in ruins? I'd seen a few century-old black-and-white photos of the house in its prime. There was one of a young Mrs. Lepp standing on the second-storey balcony looking out over her garden. It was an ornate structure painted red and blue, or so I imagined from the monochromatic photo. By the time of the fire, though, the paint had completely faded and the balcony was missing the railing. The house was attached to a long wooden barn painted white with blue trim around the windows, some of which remained up until a year ago. According to Mr. Wiebe, the roof had been rethatched as recently as the late 1970s thanks to a particularly lucrative soup and pie fundraiser. Today, though, all that remained was an eerie outline of the building and a pile of blackened rubble in the darkness and moonlight. There were no streetlights on this section of the road, just overgrown weeds on the wet, dewy lawn and a few rodents that we hoped were squirrels rustling about in the debris.

When Katie indicated that the coast was clear, I pulled back the weeds and revealed the sign. There was some information, barely legible, about the pioneering Lepps and the type of chickens they raised, which were renowned throughout the region. I gripped the right side of the sign firmly in my hands and leaned towards it; Randall took the left. Then he counted, "*Eent, twee, dree,*" and we slammed ourselves into it like big, greasy linebackers, even though we both were rather small, greasy ghostwriters. Randall made an odd wheezing sound when he did this, air exploding from his chest, and I gave him a look urging him to keep quiet. We tried again, and this time he made an even louder noise and I was beginning to wonder whether he was doing it on purpose. After two more tries, the sign was still rather *scheef*, but I didn't want to risk any further thrusting.

"It's good enough," I said.

It looked nice, or at least better, and was now clearly visible from the street, or would be in the morning when the sun came up. Then Brenda from Loans, assuming the coast was now clear, pulled out another cigarette, but before she lit it, Katie reminded her we still had one more sign to do. We were heading to Randall's mother's place and despite the late hour, there were no guarantees she'd be asleep.

"She stays up late watching infomercials," Randall

said. "I sure hope she hasn't fallen for another pyramid scheme."

We walked in the middle of the street, avoiding the empty lots which were so full of overgrown weeds that Randall was worried about poison ivy. It wasn't too far—only a few blocks away—and there was no chance of any vehicular traffic this late, so long as we avoided the cruiser strip on Sunset.

The Hiebert housebarn is in relatively good shape considering its age. This is probably due to the fact that it is still occupied. The roof on the barn is intact and the trim on the balcony had been freshly painted a bright green, like the grass that surrounds the property. It also has electricity and a satellite dish hidden around the back so it isn't too easily seen from the street.

Brenda from Loans and Katie once again offered to stand guard, but Randall thought it wasn't necessary since it was his mother's house and if anyone drove by he could say he was being a good son and helping his mother with a few chores. Brenda from Loans said doing chores at midnight wasn't the most plausible of explanations.

"If you think it would be more believable," Randall said, "we could wait a few hours, until four or so, and then I could claim I was up early helping with the milking."

Katie pointed out that the Hieberts didn't have a milking cow and hadn't had one in at least ten years.

"Besides," she said, "if anyone comes by, we'll have just as much reason to question why they're out so late as they will to question us, right?"

Brenda from Loans thought that maybe Katie and I could stand guard and she and Randall could do the thrusting and I was about to object, but then Katie nudged me and I finally caught wind of what was happening, or perhaps, what Katie was orchestrating. I'm not sure Randall had any clue, though.

"Let's get this show on the road," Katie said. She sounded like Mr. Vogt when she said it.

The whole thing made me nervous and not least of all because it took Randall and Brenda from Loans six or seven heavy, panting shoves to get the sign straight and Randall kept bellowing out like he was tossing horseshoes. After each thrust, he'd mutter Plautdietsch swear words under his breath as if he'd just narrowly missed getting a ringer.

With all the commotion, it didn't take long before Mrs. Hiebert—that's Randall's mother—ushered us inside to have some midnight peppernuts. She was wearing a pink housecoat and giant fluffy slippers to keep her feet warm on the cold floors of her housebarn.

The floor creaked as we walked and the whole place had a pleasant musty smell that reminded me of my childhood. It was exactly how a hundred-and-thirty-year-old building should smell: like a century and a half of baked bread and freshly picked flowers on the windowsill. There were no hallways. One room led directly into another and the old brick woodstove at the centre of the house heated the whole building.

"Peppernuts for everyone," Mrs. Hiebert said, only she used the Plautdietsch word, and placed one in each of our hands like we were children in the lobby at church. "One for you, Timothy. And Katie, of course." She looked at Brenda. "And you must be...?"

"I'm Brenda," she said.

"Ah, yes, from Loans," she said, handing her a pepper-nut. "I've heard so much about you. Always the best rates."

Then she gave Randall a whole bag of the tiny cookies and said he should distribute them whenever any one of us looked a bit peckish.

We were all grateful for the treats, but I swear there must have been something a bit more potent than all-spice and cloves in Mrs. Hiebert's peppernuts because out of nowhere, Randall was transformed into Mr. Stand-Up Comedian. I'd never seen him like this. He kept telling jokes that weren't very funny and required an extensive knowledge of Plautdietsch, such as the one about how the cook and the cat were never hungry, and the one about the long-neck butter-licker. I hadn't heard him tell a Plautdietsch joke in years, but he had Brenda from Loans laughing so hard that Mrs. Hiebert had to tell everyone to be *müstjestell* and keep it down.

"We don't want to wake up Mr. Hiebert," she said, who was only a few metres away in the barn on the other side of the wall, which is where he'd been relegated to ever since the divorce. "He's got a nice, comfortable set-up over there. He likes to watch those shows about people in Nevada who take old John Deere tractors and make them look brand new."

The very usable door between the house and barn indicated that their marital separation was not quite as permanent as their divorce papers implied. In fact, if the rumours were to be believed, Mrs. Hiebert would invite Mr. Hiebert for a late-night visit on special occasions. I'm not sure how this rumour began because, as far as I knew, the town surveillance system did not actually enter private residences. Perhaps it was Mr. Hiebert's cheery demeanour one Sunday that gave it away. Anyway, all of this behaviour was heavily frowned upon by both the church and by BLT who didn't want to make this type of living arrangement appear desirable.

"So, Brenda, ever tried your hand at the flying geese or drunkard's path?" Mrs. Hiebert asked.

"I'm not sure," she replied. "I think at the Ste. Adèle bar once."

Mrs. Hiebert explained that these are two of the most difficult quilting patterns, but no one seemed all that interested in discussing quilts. Mrs. Hiebert sighed.

"Here," she said, "have a look at this, since you're all interested in preservation and so on."

Mrs. Hiebert pointed to a spot on her floor where the linoleum was missing. She explained that there had been a mishap a week earlier that sent two cast-iron frying pans tumbling to the ground, damaging the flooring. This occurred while cooking *roll kuchen*, a dangerous task that involves boiling grease and often results in third-degree burns, but one that brave Edenfelders willingly suffer for the greater good of the community.

"What's that?" Katie asked.

Mrs. Hiebert pulled up a chair and, once seated, leaned down to remove more of the linoleum, revealing a beautiful, hand-painted floral pattern in red and green. Only a few inches were showing, and it had faded over time, but it was stunning nonetheless.

"Edenfeld women used to paint their floors like this," she said. "In the old days, I mean."

"I've never seen one in person before," I said.

Like the Hieberts, our floors had been covered in lino-leum as well.

"Oh, yeah, all the housebarns had them," she said.

As soon as the men had nailed down the last of the wooden floor boards and were off smoking behind the barn, Edenfeld women would painstakingly decorate the floor with bright, colourful patterns of their choice. This was a rare example of self-expression that was permitted by the church in those days. In their pallid and sober lives, here was their little splash of colour, here in the kitchen. I bet it made the food taste better too.

"Why don't you take a few photos?" Mrs. Hiebert sug-gested. "For the Preservation Society, you know?"

First, though, she made sure the door was shut between the house and the barn. There was no lock.

"Just a Plett latch," she said. Whatever that is.

Katie took the photos since she was the one who knew all about things like "aperture" and "depth of field." All I usually did was point the camera at things and press ran-dom buttons. I was told to stand by the door and make sure Mr. Hiebert didn't come barging in unexpectedly. I wasn't sure what I was supposed to do if he did.

"Get in his way," Randall said. "Distract him."

I thought that might be a better job for Randall, but he seemed preoccupied with telling Brenda from Loans a Plautdietsch joke about a sausage with two ends. It got such a big laugh from Brenda in the first go around that he told it a second time. I didn't get the joke.

"Just keep watch," he said, turning for a moment in my direction.

Katie took a few photos from a variety of angles. "I wish someone would restore these floors," she said.

It was a good idea, one that certainly warranted discussion at a future Preservation Society meeting. Unfortunately, before we could get too far into that conversation, the rumours about Mr. and Mrs. Hiebert being not quite so divorced were confirmed when Mr. Hiebert came traipsing in wearing a pair of suspenders and slacks, but no shirt. I was standing right there, but immediately made way.

"Damaging the floor again, eh?" he said. "You know, you really should be more careful."

Mrs. Hiebert stood up from her spot at the kitchen table.

"You shouldn't be here. This is not your house anymore, Rudy."

Mr. Hiebert ignored this assertion and said that if his son and his friends were taking photographs of what was below the linoleum, he had every right to be there. Of course, he had no legal right, but he had a "divine right," or so he claimed. After all, he was the one who laid the linoleum in the first place.

She tried to usher him back into the barn, but he wouldn't budge. A waft of some kind of animal smell entered the room. The barn hadn't housed animals in decades, but livestock have an aroma you can never truly remove, especially if you're like Randall's father and never really try.

Katie, who had just finished getting a few close-ups, made way as Mr. Hiebert lowered himself to the floor. He started aggressively yanking and prying off loose pieces of linoleum. Mrs. Hiebert tugged at his suspenders.

"Leave it for the professionals," she said. "Ach, Rudy, you're making it worse. Leave it alone. You might damage something."

"*Oba*, Helen, quit being such a *schwäa*!" This is a word in our language that means "festering boil." It's a local favourite.

"If there's any *schwäa* around here it's you!"

"Who are you calling a *schwäa*?"

"You just called me one, didn't you?"

I saw then why their marriage had disintegrated.

This lover's quarrel went on for quite some time, much of it in Plautdietsch, and eventually baked goods were being tossed about and Mrs. Hiebert had her shirt off too, or pretty close to it, and we figured it was time for us to vacate the premises. We didn't want to be around for the make-up romance that seemed to loom in the immediate future.

As we left, Mrs. Hiebert unhinged herself from Mr. Hiebert, scurried over to the kitchen, and handed each of us a paper bag full of peppernuts.

"For the road," she said.

We thanked her and left, stepping out into the cool night air. Katie and I went east down the middle of the street, huddling together to keep warm. Randall went west alone. His house was not far away. Brenda from Loans looked at us and looked at Randall, already halfway down the block. She stopped to light a cigarette, then bounded down the street to catch up with him. I don't know what happened after that, because Katie pulled me in the other direction towards home and made me promise I would not look back or I'd very likely be turned into a pillar of salt.

# Five

On Friday, I found an ice cream pail full of bran muffins from Mrs. Janzen on my front step. The muffins were delicious, despite the raisins, so a few days later, when I finally got to the bottom of the pail, it sure was an unpleasant surprise to find Mrs. Janzen's handwritten message explaining that she was no longer in need of my ghostwriting services. The placement of the note made me wonder just what, precisely, was in those bran muffins, but I felt no ill effects other than those one would normally feel after consuming an entire pail of bran muffins in short order and also the creeping feeling that my thriving ghostwriting career was steadily slipping away. Things were out of control and only got worse a couple days later.

I was hauling away the foundation stones of the old Friesen place when I got a phone call from the Edenfeld

Credit Union. It was Brenda from Loans. I told her I didn't have time to talk at the moment since they were expecting me at the landfill. I said I'd return her call as soon as the Thiessens finished unloading my truck. She said she knew how those boys operated and that if I could convince the three of them to stop *knack*ing *zoat* so much and speed things up it would be much appreciated. She said the matter was urgent.

On my lunch break, with my feet dangling from the back of Mr. Vogt's truck bed, I somehow found myself entangled in a conversation about nuisance beavers. The Thiessen boys had some traps over by Sandilands and Eddie said he was thinking of maybe driving out there this weekend to check on them and wondered if I, or maybe one of the Reimers, would like to go along. As much as I love a good walk in a tick-infested forest with some Thiessens, I regretfully passed on the opportunity, finished my egg salad sandwich, and, even though the beaver discussion was far from over, told the boys I needed to make a phone call.

If Brenda from Loans was calling it could only mean one thing: I had missed another mortgage payment. We'd had to decide between the mortgage and Katie's tuition for the year. At the time when we first signed on, the Edenfeld Credit Union had a rather unique procedure whereby you were automatically approved for a loan of any size so long as you could successfully recite Psalm 23 from memory. "This weeds out the undesirables," they said. BLT radically altered this practice, though, and today the only way to get a mortgage is if you agree to let the town demolish your house once they determine it's an eyesore. Lucky for us, and thanks to Katie's remarkable Bible memorization skills, we were able to extend ourselves well beyond the means of a meagre Parks and Rec income.

I briefly considered asking my parents for money, but they worry about us enough as it is. They're retired now and living in some place called Yarrow, British Columbia. They don't understand why we've decided to stay in Edenfeld when the economy is not so great and the winters are so harsh. It doesn't take much time in "Beautiful British Columbia" before Manitobans are ready to denounce their home province. You should have seen them when they came to visit us last Christmas. They nearly froze to death just getting off the plane. After that, my mother proclaimed that Christmas would be held in Yarrow from then on, but that would mean we would be the ones who'd have to fly out there and, the way things were, we couldn't afford the plane tickets.

Thankfully, Brenda's message wasn't as bad as I feared. In fact, she was weirdly unconcerned. Yes, we had missed our last mortgage payment of $950, and yes, we would need to address the matter promptly or risk further action, but she read it like a script and said that, given our impeccable track record (it wasn't all that impeccable), she was pretty certain it must have just been a mistake on our part (it wasn't) and that the whole matter could be addressed without much difficulty.

"As long as it doesn't happen again," she said, "it shouldn't be an issue."

She was more accommodating than anyone else I'd ever interacted with from the loans department before. I figured it was because we both had an affinity for Edenfeld history. Us amateur historians take care of our own.

I asked her how things were going with the Elsie Dyck house. Did she know if there had been any interested buyers and had she been able to procure the necessary funds to get a plaque put up?

She paused for a long while and then said, "Well, you know, it's a two-storey house built in the thirties."

"So that means it's a good candidate for preservation, then?" I asked.

"The attic needs updating. They've still got wood shavings up there. Costs a fortune to heat in the winter."

"Right, so just a plaque, then?"

Again, she paused, then moved the conversation in an entirely different direction. Apparently, her graciousness regarding our mortgage hiccup was not so much due to our mutual interest in becoming reacquainted with the past. Rather, she was more interested in becoming reacquainted with Randall.

"I want to get back together with him," she said.

"Back together?"

Had the two of them even been a couple? All I knew was that she'd hired Randall to write a book for her a few years back. *Fifty Shades of Grunthal*. I don't want to spoil it for you, because I'm sure you're all very eager to read it, but rest assured, there are plenty of racy scenes in a moonlit truck bed. It's no wonder she used a pen name—Jessica Pure—to keep her identity under wraps.

The whole time, though, Randall insisted everything was strictly professional between him and Brenda from Loans, but Katie has always had her suspicions. "Seems like she's into Randall," she'd say, with a curled lip and wrinkled nose. "Lord knows I don't know why." I hadn't noticed anything, but then, I'm rather oblivious to that sort of thing. Even Mrs. Agatha Warkentin's romantic interludes with Mr. George Falk at the Scrabble tournament last year went completely under my radar.

Brenda from Loans asked if I could help her out with Randall. I could talk to him. Convince him somehow. Use my powers of persuasion. Obviously she had no idea how limited those powers were.

She said she and I could have a mutually beneficial relationship.

"I'll rub your back, if you rub mine," she said.

I agreed, but desperately hoped she didn't mean it literally.

"Sure, Brenda, you can count on me."

I didn't ask what had happened that evening after we straightened the signs, but if Brenda was calling to enlist my services in setting her up with Randall, it must mean that the contact between the two of them was minimal.

I told her I'd speak with Randall. She said "good," and hung up without saying goodbye or telling me what was going to happen with the Elsie Dyck house or reminding me about our delinquent loan.

I wasn't sure what I'd say to Randall. He isn't an easy man to convince of anything, nor does he pick up on signals, and he was currently far too into Russian dating websites and brewing poor imitations of American craft beer to notice the romantic potential that lay right in front of him.

I spent the rest of the afternoon breathing the noxious fumes of the Edenfeld landfill. We were burning tractor tires. We'd been told that city people don't like tractor tire parks, so the town needed to invest in modern play structures that would bring young families in. "Once the smell of burning rubber dissipates," said Mr. Vogt, "we'll be inundated with new families from the city." We were hoping to get all the tire-free parks constructed before the end of summer so the Faith Barn folks could give them a test run during their Sunday school kickoff event in early September. And, despite the black smoke filling my lungs, I felt hopeful for a moment. Soon it would be fall, when the grain is harvested and the pigs are slaughtered and Edenfelders are rolling in cash and everyone is in a good and generous mood, even towards ghostwriters.

It seemed the good and generous mood started early because that Tuesday night, after a screening of *The Organists of Osterwick: A Love Story*, the Preservation Society passed around a hat, scrounged up nearly three hundred bucks, and voted unanimously to hire me to write a book about Edenfeld's history.

"This should get you started," Mr. Wiebe said.

"Uh, thanks, I think."

It was Brenda from Loans's idea and I couldn't help but wonder if it was some sort of bribe to further convince me to talk to Randall. Or maybe she was trying to help me pay my mortgage. I wasn't sure. Considering the size of the task, it wasn't a lot of money, but then, I wasn't going to turn it down either, even though a large chunk of the payment was in gift cards for cottage cheese perogies. They said that more than eighty people had put their names on a list, saying they would be willing to purchase a copy of the book if and when it became available.

"Half the profits you can keep," said Mr. Wiebe, "and

the other half will go towards plaques, like the one for Elsie Dyck's house."

Mrs. Ens said the business model was flawed considering that many of those eighty names were well into their nineties. "How many will still be alive by the time this book is published?" she wondered.

No one had written an Edenfeld history book in nearly fifty years, and even that one was quite niche. I have a copy of it in my collection. It's called *Edenfeld: A Town of a Thousand Horses*. That's the English title, anyway. Of course, much has changed since then, including, but not limited to, a vast reduction in horses.

"The idea is to tell the story of Edenfeld from 1876 to the present day with pictures and charts and maps of all the places where things used to be and aren't anymore," explained Mrs. Friesen. "That shouldn't be too difficult for you. You could include photographs, like the ones of the floors in the Hiebert housebarn, and flesh out the rest with a bit of research."

It's true that I had written plenty of books for plenty of local people, but picking and choosing the most important people and places from all these volumes was going to be quite the task. There was always some debate about the precise location of the Bartsch creamery on Main Street, or in what year the elders forced the old silent movie theatre to shut down, or whether it had been R.F. Klassen or R.P. Klassen who had first owned the hatchery, and whether the Rempel store should actually be considered Edenfeld's first business, "especially when you consider the fact that Mr. Rempel had come under the influence of the *Bruderthaler*." I knew all about these debates. The books I'd ghostwritten contained plenty of contradictions. Each person had their own version of things and sometimes even their own timeline of events. It was going to be messy and I knew that I would never please everyone. Before I had a chance to openly indicate my hesitation, however, Mrs. Friesen made eye contact with me.

"It could save the town," she said.

"*Oba*, Sarah, I think you might be overstating it a bit, don't you think?" said Mrs. Ens.

"No, it's important," said Mrs. Friesen. "I really think you should do this, Timothy. Just keep it under your hat for now. Better to ask forgiveness than permission."

Katie said neither forgiveness nor permission would be sought. She wanted me to write the book. And, despite my worries, so did I. I wanted to rebel, at least in some way. The task was not without risks, however. After all, around here, writers tend to go missing. Elsie Dyck is only the most well-known example of this phenomenon. You don't even have to be famous. It's happened to three of my clients already. They print a few copies of the local history book I wrote for them and then, without fail, some old man gets upset because the book downplays the role of the Driedger clan in the Edenfeld revival movement of the 1960s or what have you, and the next thing you know, the author—or, I should say, the person with their name on the cover—is living with their spinster aunts somewhere on the other side of the river. This place is like a Bermuda Triangle for writers, which is why I've always stuck to ghostwriting. Better to be on the safe side.

I requested that the Edenfeld book be officially credited to the Preservation Society as a whole, rather than singling me out for recognition or reprisal. No need to have my name on it—that's what I was used to. There was even some discussion of making the whole book a collective effort.

"We could each write a chapter and that way no one person will take the blame," said Mr. Wiebe.

"Like the ending to *Murder on the Orient Express*?" Katie asked.

Those who'd read the book said it was a great analogy, and those who hadn't begged the others to explain, but they adamantly refused, saying that it would spoil the whole thing.

In the end, Mrs. Friesen argued that this Agatha Christie nonsense was far too complicated and that I should work alone. She was confident in my abilities and said it would be a mess if they all got involved. She easily brought Mrs. Ens on board when she reminded her of the complete disaster that was the South Edenfeld Women's Ministry *somma borscht* at last year's Sunday school picnic. There was no need for any more discussion after that. I had a book to write.

# Hoafst

# Six

They were slaughtering a pig on one of the empty lots on Main Street. It's an annual fall tradition, and usually something I avoid, but I was on my way to the library to use the computers and there was no way to get there without either trespassing through Mrs. Unrau's petunias and risking her wrath or traversing within proximity of the annual pig slaughter.

A crowd had gathered. Clowns were making balloon animals and there was a game for the children to play that involved running around in circles pretending not to dance. You could even get your face painted. This year BLT thought the event needed some pizazz, so he hired a country cover band and approved the sale of light beer. I wasn't entirely convinced alcohol should be added to the scenario, but BLT thought it would "attract a younger crowd."

Anyway, once the pig bits were all divvied up, you could stick around for the roast and enjoy some mustard-heavy potato salad on the side. I figured I might come back later.

A young couple was standing outside the Elsie Dyck house when I walked past. I didn't recognize them and assumed they were from out of town. Sometimes the more adventurous city people come out here to watch us butcher the hogs. The photos get a lot of likes on social media. This couple, though, had strayed away from the festivities, and I became curious when I noticed a pamphlet in the woman's hand. *A Historic Walking Tour of Edenfeld*. I had no idea how they got one of those and wondered aloud whether they should be displaying it quite so openly.

"Where'd you get that?" I asked.

"At the library," the woman said.

That couldn't possibly be true.

"You mean the church, perhaps?" I asked. "South Edenfeld?"

She whispered something to her partner.

"No, I'm pretty sure it was the library," she said. "That old building on the corner over there."

They stood shivering on the cracked sidewalk in front of the house and took a few pictures. The place was still for sale, but this couple, barely in their twenties, seemed more interested in selfies than real estate. I was curious to see how up to date their pamphlet was, but I hadn't brought along my black felt marker to make any necessary deletions.

As I turned to walk away, the woman, still holding the pamphlet, asked, "Was this where Elsie Dyck lived?"

"Yeah, I think so," I said.

"You'd think there would at least be a plaque or something."

The couple looked at the map, then back up at the house. Whoever was inside closed the curtains and turned on the front porch lights. It was the middle of the day.

"553 Melrose," she muttered, before positioning her partner squarely in front of the building and removing her gloves to take another photo. He held a book in front of him, then posed like it was for the cover of *Gentlemen's Quarterly*.

They remarked that they needed to pick up a scarf or a toque or something while they were here because they hadn't dressed for the chill and asked where such items could be procured in our fair town. They had failed to locate the megamart earlier in the day.

"For a small town, the roads sure are confusing," she said.

"Yeah, sorry about that," I said, as if the street names were my fault. "Megamart Way leads nowhere."

I pointed them in the direction of the thrift store.

They seemed like a nice enough couple and I thought about offering to take a picture of the two of them together, but got nervous when I saw a few old men wearing sunglasses sitting in lawn chairs across the street. They were drinking coffee, the steam rising in front of them, and staring in our direction. So I just kept on walking towards the Dick Plett Library.

If I was going to write an Edenfeld book, I figured the library was the best place to start, especially if they were now handing out historic walking tour brochures like it was no big deal. I still had my doubts about that.

The library is in a pretty sad state. It's actually been on our preservation list for quite some time, but as with many of the buildings on that list, we're largely powerless to prevent its decay. It's right on the preferred route for hauling junk to the landfill and the Tyndall stone has turned black from years of neglect. Originally, it was called Edenfeld Public Library, but after all three Ls fell off the sign they decided to rename it after a former town treasurer, whose association with the aggressive distribution of Gideon Bibles was seen as a significant contribution to the promotion of literacy in the region. WELCOME TO THE DICK PLETT LIBRARY the sign says. Below it a banner reads: *Come Try Our Personal Computers*. It's hung there like that for almost thirty years.

Two tall trees stood on either side of the front steps. Their leaves had fallen already, as had a few branches that I kicked out of my way to open the door. It was dark inside—a few bulbs were burnt out—and I entered reluctantly, but I had a task to complete. Research. I hadn't been to the library in about a year and was shocked to see the decline. Struck by the smell of mould, I looked up. The roof was leaking and there were buckets placed every few metres to catch the excess. Signs along the wall pointed in the direction of the computer room, which was the only section of the library that seemed to be well-lit and in good repair. I glanced at the old woman who stood at the door waiting with bated breath to show some young folks how one of these "personal computers" worked.

"Where do you keep the pamphlets?" I asked.

"Oh, you mean like gospel tracts?"

"Not exactly. *A Historic Walking Tour of Edenfeld?*" I asked. "Someone told me you were handing those out ..."

She turned on one of the computers and wiped the dusty monitor with a wet cloth.

"Oh, no, I certainly don't think we'd have anything like that," she said.

"Well, I was told ..."

"You must have been misinformed," she said. "Would you like me to show you how the personal computer works?"

I didn't need her help, but I did need access to the computers. Katie and I had to cancel our high-speed Internet a while ago to save some money. I wasn't even able to use my phone. Not properly, anyway. Not for the Internet. My screen was almost cracked beyond use and Katie's didn't look so great either after a particularly heated discussion about Jacques Derrida with one of her classmates. Going offline was a tough decision, but Katie said she could use the computers at the university and I could make do by stealing the Wi-Fi at Ernie's and checking out these world-renowned beauties right here at the Dick Plett Library. It would save us seventy dollars a month.

"You know, we had personal computers here before anyone else in town," the woman said. "It was one of our mayor's initiatives."

It's true. For about ten years, the library was the only place in Edenfeld where you could use the Internet. In the early days, women would sneak off and look up recipes for *niejoahschkuake* while their husbands were reading back issues of the *Manitoba Co-operator*, and when the wives were distracted, say, while browsing the bountiful collection of *Crochet World,* the husbands darted over to the computers to look up pictures of Mennonite women exposing their ankles.

She reached over me and demonstrated how to move the mouse and open up the web browser. Then she moved the cursor to the search bar and told me I could type in absolutely anything and see what came up.

"It's amazing. You can get recipes, scripture verses, pictures of cats, anything," she said. "You can even check your credit union balance."

I told her I most certainly would not be doing that.

She asked for photo ID and said I had to sign a consent form and promise not to complain or write an angry letter to the board if I discovered anything that might shatter my concept of the world. I told her there was nothing to worry about in that regard and filled in my information on the clipboard she handed me: *Timothy Heppner, Edenfeld, Manitoba.*

"Oh, a local boy."

She took a seat at the computer and then, one letter at a time, typed in a password that would give me access to the "World Wide Web." I saw that it was "Edenfeld1876" but pretended I hadn't been looking. By the time she was done entering it into the computer, the whole thing froze up and she spun around on her rolling chair.

"Dorothy, come help!"

A woman yelled from another room, saying that she was on her way and that no one should get their *unjat-jleedinj* in a twist. Moments later, Dorothy entered. I'd seen her at the library before. She was about the same age as the first librarian but had a blue streak in her hair and thick gold bracelets on her arms. Her T-shirt said *Literature is Life.*

"What have you done now, Agnes?"

They argued and kept bumping each other out of the chair to try a few things because the other one wasn't doing it right. Dorothy told Agnes that this was exactly why she didn't want computers at the library in the first place, but Agnes pointed at me and said I wouldn't even have paid the library a visit if they didn't have them.

"Why don't you try this?" I said, reaching around back to turn the whole thing off and then on again. A few seconds later, the computer rebooted and everything appeared to be functional.

"Well done, young man," Agnes said. "You should work at the library."

She was thoroughly exhausted by this time and decided to take a break in the staff room where she said she'd do some knitting. She left me alone with Dorothy, who stood behind me and looked over my shoulder, eagerly anticipating my next move.

"Thanks, I think I'll be okay," I said.

When she was certain that Agnes was at the other end of the building, she leaned over and said, "You were interested in Edenfeld, were you not?"

I looked at her, puzzled.

"I overheard you asking about it."

She lowered her volume even further.

"You won't find much on these things," she said. "Just try."

I went to the web browser, just like Agnes had so ably instructed me, and typed in the word "Edenfeld." However, that didn't seem specific enough, since there were so many villages with that name, so I typed "Edenfeld, Manitoba" and added the word "people" so I'd get some interesting pictures.

"See what I mean?" she said.

I couldn't believe it. Oh, there were photos all right, but not what I was expecting. Whenever I looked up Edenfeld on my home computer, I would find dozens of pictures of men with long beards and black suits and women in long dresses and black bonnets. Butter churning. Horse-drawn buggies. You know, the photogenic Mennonites. Not that most people around here live like that, of course, but when tourists come to town, they don't bother with the assimilated Mennos driving minivans and wearing Lululemons. Instead, when they aren't standing disappointedly in front of Elsie Dyck's house, they go "Mennonite spotting." They wait in front of the thrift store, sometimes for hours, until they spot a woman in a kerchief to put on their travel blog. There, on the computers at the Dick Plett Library, however, all those pictures were gone. Blocked. Blacked out with an $X$. In their place was an entirely different kind of misrepresentation.

"Last summer Mayor Wiens sent us to sit at the patio at that new pizza place out on the highway and take pictures of all the young people enjoying adult beverages," Dorothy explained. "He posted them online. Got some kid from the city to make sure they show up in the search results. For some reason, the mayor was particularly interested in getting photographs of anyone wearing cut-off jean shorts."

I could see that the computers would get me nowhere, so I asked Dorothy if they had any local history books and she led me to a shelf in the far corner of the library against the back wall.

"We used to have a lot more," she said, "before Agnes was put in charge."

In front of the shelf were three large buckets nearly over-flowing with water from the leaking roof and they could have used at least one more. By then, Agnes was back from her break. It seemed awfully short, hardly enough time to get a lot of knitting done, but she announced that it was now Dorothy's turn for a break. They argued. Eventually Dorothy left, but made it quite clear that she had no inten-tion of fixing Agnes's knitting errors.

Agnes was none too pleased that I'd abandoned my spot at the computer.

"What do you want in this section?" she asked. "There's nothing good here."

I could see that already, but intended to browse the selection anyway. It was just too bad there were all these buckets in my path.

"Can I empty these for you?" I asked. "I work for Parks and Rec."

"No, no. Abe will come later and do it," she said.

"But this one's almost full and—"

"Abe will do it."

I positioned myself between the buckets, careful not to knock them over, and perused the shelf for anything of value. There wasn't much. All I found was a book-on-tape version of *Letters to the Editor: The Collected Writings of Ruth F. Quiring* and a beat-up copy of *The Seven Habits of Highly Effective Mennonites*. I scanned the table of con-tents. The habits included attending evening services, milking cows, and consuming large quantities of sausage. Transformative literature. I decided to take it. Sometimes I select books out of sympathy. When they keep track—if anyone keeps track—I want the record to show that someone had an interest in such things. I like the idea of throwing off the statistics.

The microfiche didn't produce much of use either. According to Agnes, all the local history books were removed during the Great Edenfeld Library Cull of '96.

"We made a lot of progress in those days. Completely got rid of every non-English book we had."

Officially, they were clearing up space for "contemporary works that will be appealing to young people," such as the New Testament with cartoon pictures of Lazarus and books about the dangers of listening to rap music. Unofficially, though, the goal was to rid the library of anything that might document the lives of Edenfelders prior to BLT Wiens's miraculous transformation of the town into the "modern metropolis we know and love today."

"Is this really all you have?" I asked.

"You'd have much better luck with the computers," she said.

I took my book and exited the building. Compared to the dingy interior of the library, outside was shockingly bright and sunny. As soon as my eyes adjusted to the light, I saw that there they were again, those men in sunglasses. They'd moved their lawn chairs and were now perched right across from the library. They were still drinking coffee and one of them was gnawing well into the green part of a slice of watermelon. They stared straight ahead and said nothing, which was strange, because old men in

Edenfeld are usually yelling things from across the road. Their silence was unsettling, so I quickly made my way out of the neighbourhood. When I passed Melrose Avenue, I stopped.

"*Diewel!*"

I'd never actually signed out the book that was now in my possession. I reckoned that stealing from the library was probably not one of the habits of highly effective Mennonites. I was ashamed, but also hungry. I would return it some other time.

At the pig slaughter, I was propositioned by a clown who explained he'd run out of children to paint and wondered whether I'd like either Batman or Jesus on my face. I declined both offers. Instead, I picked up some roast pork on a bun, which they were giving away for free. Well, actually, City Sheila was there taking donations and giving away sample-sized mascara, but in the minds of a lot of Edenfelders, this meant everything was complimentary. I threw a few quarters in the bucket, quickly, and in such a manner that she wouldn't see the modest size of my donation.

"What are you reading?" she asked.

I showed her the book and she complimented me on my fine choice. She offered a free mascara sample for Katie, which I accepted as I reached for the condiments. When I did, something fell from the book to the ground, a pamphlet that I instantly recognized. *A Historic Walking Tour of Edenfeld.* I scooped it up, hoping it wouldn't be noticed and said I had to take my bun and run, even though, much to City Sheila's bemusement, I hadn't adequately layered it with barbecue sauce.

When I was a safe distance away, I flipped it open to the map. It seemed up to date; all the Xs in all the right places. Someone had stuffed it into my stolen book. Highly effective indeed.

Soon after, I got a text from Randall. It was hard to read through the cracked screen, but I made out that it was nothing urgent, a message about a new IPA made with sorrel he was trying. He also wanted to know what the going rate was these days for housebarns. "Just the barn part," he'd written. He was asking for his dad. I texted back that I had absolutely no idea. I told him about the book with the pamphlet inside and he replied, "Yeah, that Dorothy is a loose cannon. You better be careful." Randall said he'd be praying for me and even though I wasn't sure if he meant it, I thanked him and told him I'd be praying for him too, which in Edenfeld is about as sincere and automatic a reply as "fine" is to "how are you?" I thought about mentioning Brenda from Loans, but still didn't know what I was supposed to say, exactly, so I kept it to myself and added it to my mental list of things in both our lives that could use some divine intervention.

On my way home, I cut through the neighbour's backyard and looked up at our big old elm, its branches beginning to shed and stretched out over the yard like arms. I liked the sound of the leaves under my feet and was in no hurry to rake them up, even though the Bergens constantly complained. We'd been reported twice already, once for not shovelling our sidewalk and another time for the infrequency of our mowing, and I was concerned we'd get a third call soon about the leaves. I knew the guy at the town office who made those phone calls, though, and I'd always been able to win some extra time in the past. He really likes it when I let him beat me at crokinole. Do that and I could have all the time I wanted with my out-of-control thistles.

I entered through the back door. All the lights were off. There was a note on the counter from Katie saying she was in the city using the personal computers with the high-speed Internet connection they've got at the university. She mentioned that she'd made some *kjielkje* earlier and that there was still some left in the fridge, ready to be heated up. Then it said, *I hope you make a lot of progress on your book today, Timothy.* There were three hearts and a tiny flower that she always drew next to her signature, which she had altered this time to resemble the flowers on the Hiebert's floor. I heated up the *kjielkje* in a bowl, added some ketchup, then laid out on the couch with my feet up and my Internet-less computer on my lap.

I opened the pamphlet I'd found in the library book and compared it to my original copy. A perfect match. The walking tour of Edenfeld is a short one these days, if you're looking for existing buildings, that is. I turned on my laptop and made a list of all the landmarks mentioned therein, including the x-ed out ones. I listed every demolished building, every levelled orchard, and every historic site that was now known only by a plaque. "On this parking lot once stood the famous Rempel store." I also included fifteen housebarns, two windmills, one machine shop, the old hotel on Main Street, and the three churches that shut down due to declining attendance; people left in droves because they weren't keeping up with the times and using overhead projectors. It didn't take long before

I'd written the first twenty pages of the book, in list form, mind you, and full of typos, but it was a good start. I knew I had to stop for the evening when I'd documented every building mentioned on the walking tour. Also, my supply of *kjielkje* had run dry.

What would I call the book, though? I typed "THE UNAUTHORIZED HISTORY OF EDENFELD, MANITOBA." I stared at the screen for a while, wondering where I would go from there. "THE UNAUTHORIZED HISTORY OF EDENFELD, MANITOBA by Timothy Heppner." I sighed, held down the backspace button until my name was gone, and closed the laptop. Then I went outside to clean up the leaves.

# Seven

Katie says it's absolutely impossible to get from Edenfeld to Altfeld without getting a couple stone chips in the windshield, even if you go as slow as Edenfelders do during their Sunday after-church drives. "And a few on the way back too," she says.

I'm always nervous about that thirty-kilometre stretch and asked her to keep it under fifty. Maybe then there'd be less impact when the stones struck. However, Katie is an experienced gravel road driver and said we didn't have time for my overly cautious ways.

When the first truck whipped past us, she skillfully swerved out of the path of the oncoming shrapnel. A plume of dust enveloped the road and I was thankful I'd remembered to keep the windows closed.

"Gosh, if they don't want to pave it, I wish they'd at least spray on a layer of oil to keep the dust down."

It didn't take long before another pickup truck roared by and machine-gunned us with gravel. This time, however, Katie couldn't avoid the onslaught and pulled over to inspect the damage.

"*Dietschlaund*! Looks pretty bad," I said. "Probably one of the Thiessen boys. I think BLT pays them to do this."

Katie said I was being paranoid and that driving up and down gravel roads was exactly the sort of thing the Thiessen boys were likely to do in their spare time.

"They do it for free," she said.

Despite the stone chip, we were not deterred. We were on our way to one of the classical music concerts Altfelders like to host in their largest barn loft. Sometimes they even have jazz or some talented pianist will come in from the city and play Shostakovich's Piano Concerto No. 2 in F Major. That's what the poster said, anyway. Not that they let Altfelders put up posters anywhere in Edenfeld—there's a strictly enforced civic bylaw against it—but Katie just happened to stumble across one at a highway gas station on her way to class. We don't promote Altfeld in Edenfeld. We're not even supposed to buy their frozen turkeys. BLT once mailed a vaguely xenophobic letter to everyone in town, compelling us all to "unite in the war against out-of-town turkeys." The mayor is threatened by Altfeld, its proximity to the city, and the fact it's also in the running to get a big-box store. He keeps the road between the towns extra gravelly.

Katie, however, thinks the gravel roads are a blessing. She claims they've protected Altfeld from the land developers.

"Altfeld is not a bedroom community. It's not trying to be a suburb. It's its own thing," she says. "Complain all you want, Timothy, but I hope these roads never get paved."

I once asked Katie if she'd ever consider moving back there. Maybe we could get a housebarn ourselves and live a quiet, peaceful existence in Altfeld, but she said she wanted to stay right where she was in Edenfeld.

"I like the fight," she said.

We needed a break, and an inexpensive one. Shostakovich. I wasn't sure who that was. Randall said he knew all about him since he knows "all things Russian," but said there was no way he was going to take his Audi to Altfeld. Katie figured if an eminent pianist was coming in all the way from the city to perform a Shostakovich concerto for us country folk, it would be nice if a few of us showed up. The tickets were ten dollars or eight if you bought them in advance, but that would have meant an extra trip out to Altfeld to get them, and that was more than our windshield could handle.

Katie brought along a few bottles of beer, which she tossed onto my lap to hold as we drove.

"They'll probably explode if we put them in the back," she said.

The beer was one of Randall's thick, black concoctions which Katie had developed a taste for. I pointed out that the Shostakovich poster never mentioned it was a BYOB event.

"You could at least pour it into an empty Pepsi bottle and pretend," I said.

"Relax, Timothy. It'll be fine."

When we arrived, our truck was coated in a thick layer

of dust, and a young boy motioned for us to pull into the outdoor skating rink to park. Then a man, presumably his father, offered to fix our stone chip. They fill it with some kind of liquid that hardens and then everything is as good as new in a few minutes.

"We do epoxy here," he said, adding that it was the best method of repair.

I took his word for it. It didn't take him long and I offered to pay him for his services, but he explained that wouldn't be necessary, saying something about how insurance would cover it. Then he told me to enjoy the Shostakovich.

"Will do," I said, far from confident.

I was tentative about entering the barn, but Katie marched in, beer in tow, and handed the woman at the door some cash. She stamped our hands with a red smiley face and we made our way up to the loft where we plopped down on some cheap plastic chairs that bowed when we sat in them. They had popcorn and oatmeal raisin cookies and Styrofoam coffee cups that "could be used however you please." When Katie cracked open the bottles, I turned around to see if anyone was looking. They were.

"Cheers," they said and hoisted their beverages.

Katie poured Randall's beer into the cups and even wrote our names on them with a blue ink pen. *Timothy Heppner. Katie Brandt-Heppner.*

"That way they won't get mixed up with anyone else's."

I threw a stir stick in mine. I wasn't used to this kind of thing.

The first performer was one of the Sunday school girls from down the road who plunked away at "My Anchor

Holds" while an old man, probably her grandfather, accompanied her on the banjo. They did an eclectic mix of songs, including crowd favourites like "Brown Eyed Girl" and "Proud Mary," and an old woman with an out-of-tune mandolin and out-of-control vibrato joined in for one of them, which was less adorable, but still had its appeal. When they got to the end of "Sweetly Resting" the trio sat down and there was enthusiastic applause from the audience.

After that, there was a fifteen-minute break so we could buy merchandise or risk wood ticks while relieving our bladders in the tall grass behind the barn. The whole Shostakovich thing was a fundraiser to repair the foundation for one of the barns. Rather than tearing the building down, the town had decided to come together, drink some beer, listen to music most of them didn't fully understand or appreciate, and eat baked goods dipped in corn syrup.

The audience was typical for Altfeld. Men with long beards and suspenders sat next to women in ripped jeans and tank tops, and people wore makeup or didn't, and people had their heads covered or didn't, and people slept in on Sunday or got up early to milk the cows before church, and all these people seemed to get along and tolerate Shostakovich.

When the pianist finished there was a standing ovation. It was an impressive performance, despite the fact that a loud, giant oscillating fan kept blowing against her sheet music and a teenage boy had to sit there and hold down the papers the whole time. Still, the Altfelders clapped loud and long and at the end of the evening a woman stood up and announced that the event had raised enough money to get the barn repair started.

She mentioned that if they really wanted to get that barn repaired fast—if people really wanted to make a difference—they should pick up a copy of the Altfeld book on their way out. A young man with his fingernails painted black and a swath of hair covering one eye was sitting at the merchandise table selling them. He handled the money while an elderly woman recorded the names and email addresses of anyone interested in getting on their mailing list for information about upcoming events where soup and/or pie would be consumed. I looked the boy right in his one eye and handed him a twenty.

"And five's your change," he said. "I hope you enjoy it. It's a great book."

He opened it up and offered to sign it.

"I wrote chapter six," he said. "2010 to the present day."

I let him put his name down and thanked him. The book was called *The Altfeld Book: 140 Years, 140 Editions.* Apparently it gets an annual update. If someone moves to town and stays for any length of time, they add them to the new edition, and if you go to university or marry a Schmidt or birth a calf, all of this is documented and preserved and sold at a reasonable cost to enthusiastic locals. There was a map showing the town in 1880 and another from just last year. They were side by side for comparison. Some things had changed, of course, but in many ways, Altfeld of the twenty-first century looked much the same as it did when our ancestors first fled the old country for this new, colder, swampier one. The Ginters still lived where the Ginters had lived since the 1800s, right next to the Hamms, and although the barn on the Bestvater yard had been expanded and the chicken coop moved to make way for more rhubarb plants, the town had managed to preserve itself. It was like an open-air museum, but people lived in all the buildings and they didn't charge admission and some of them painted their fingernails black.

After the concert, we stopped by Katie's grandmother's place. It was late, well past nine o'clock, but she was up. Somehow she knew we'd be there. Her house was only a few doors down from the barn, and she was sitting on her front lawn in a chair, wearing a thick sweater and drinking yerba mate while she waited for the concert to be over.

"I can hear it all perfectly fine from here," she said. "No need to climb those stairs."

She had also saved herself eight dollars.

Usually we visit on Sundays and she feeds us fruit-filled *vereniki* and green bean soup and then Katie and I mow the lawn and trim the hedges. She lives on a giant property with a few goats and a donkey to keep the coyotes away and it's all too much work for one person of her vintage. All her other grandchildren live much farther away, in Hochstadt and Neuschanzenthal and La Crete.

"I've heard about that Shostakovich," Grandma Brandt said. "Had a heck of a time with that Stalin character now, didn't he?"

"I really wouldn't know ..."

She invited us in because we were standing there pretending not to shiver. She had been sitting there for hours and wasn't at all taken aback by the impending winter.

"I see you've got *The Altfeld Book*," she said. "Is that the latest edition?"

"Yeah, well, I can't pass up a local history book."

"I'm on page one-thirteen," she said. "Katie's in there too."

I flipped to the page and there they were, Grandma Brandt picking beets and Katie, a toddler, holding the ice cream pail for her.

"Cute picture," I said.

"I hear you're writing one about Edenfeld," Grandma Brandt said.

"You heard about that?" I asked.

"Word gets around," she said. "How do you have time for that with all the other writing you do?"

I hesitated.

"He doesn't really have any ghostwriting clients at the moment," Katie said.

"That's not true. I have a couple left," I said.

I still had two projects remaining. One was a Bible commentary for a retired reverend and the other was a collection of poems about *borscht* for Mrs. Esau. I convinced her I was capable of writing poetry by reciting a few psalms and a handful of proverbs and since she'd never actually read any poetry herself, she thought it was all pretty good.

> *Borscht* how I love thee,
> Let me count the ways.
> Oh that I could eat you,
> Never ceasing for days.

I paused. "Yeah, time is not an issue."

Then Katie's grandmother asked that since we had so much time on our hands, perhaps we wouldn't mind stopping by again on the weekend because the *fate hahn* in front of her house needed picking.

"It's delicious," she said, "but a real nuisance when it gets in the cracks of your sidewalk."

There were also a few burned-out lightbulbs and she wasn't tall enough to reach them without standing on a stool. I told her I could replace them right then and there, but she said she was all out of bulbs and wondered whether we could bring some with us the next time we came. Edenfeld may have convenient access to lightbulbs, but there were more than a few things, I figured, that it lacked. I threw *The Altfeld Book* in the back seat as we left.

"In case we're pulled over," I told Katie.

"Oh, please," she said and fetched the book, cradling it in her lap like the booze we'd taken with us earlier.

Katie said she'd had a bit too much of Randall's home-brew and I should drive. I needed practice on gravel roads anyway, she said.

The whole drive back to Edenfeld, she put her bare feet up on the dash and paged through the book while I weaved back and forth to the good side of the road, some-times veering almost into the ditch to avoid the worst of the washboard surface.

By the time we'd pulled into the driveway, Katie said she'd read through the whole thing. What she meant was that she had glanced at every page.

"And look, Timothy," she said. "All the authors' names are right here on the cover."

"I know. One of them even signed it," I said. "He also gave me this business card in case I'm ever in the market for a new skateboard."

Katie unlocked the front door and flipped on the light switch.

"They're not afraid, Timothy," she said, then wandered over to the office and placed *The Altfeld Book* on my desk. "For inspiration."

# Eight

Every year, sometime between the pig slaughter and
Christmas, Edenfelders sell cheap used books at the
Golden Slumbers Retirement Manor. In the early days,
the manor had trouble getting occupants since word got
out that it was named after a Beatles song, but over time
people forgot all about John Lennon's "bigger than Jesus"
comments and now the place is bursting at the seams. I
was hoping I'd have better luck here than at the library,
but even if I didn't, I had no choice but to attend the sale.
Brenda from Loans had called again asking whether I had
spoken to Randall yet and, with our mortgage teetering on
the edge of foreclosure, I told her I'd be meeting Randall
at Golden Slumbers. I knew he was usually in a receptive
mood when surrounded by the printed word.

The Golden Slumbers sale is usually where you can

find all those local books written long before Randall and I ever got into the ghostwriting business. When it says Mrs. Annie Plett on the cover, you really can trust that Mrs. Annie Plett herself actually wrote it. They also sell handmade doilies and toy tractors, but Katie and I tend to gravitate towards the literature. It's a good thing Edenfeld seniors let the books go for next to nothing, because with our Wi-Fi cancelled, we don't have enough reading material to get us through the next few months and we'll have to spend all those cold winter nights huddled up playing Dutch Blitz or something.

To come away with anything worthwhile at Golden Slumbers, you have to sift through thousands of Amish romance novels and glossy coffee-table books about Princess Diana. I'm usually up to the task, though, and this year, I made a list of what I was looking for: local histories and biographies, theological treatises, edgy Mennonite literature. You know, the good stuff. I thought there might be an item or two that could help me write the Edenfeld book, or add to it, anyway. I certainly wasn't lacking in source material. My friends in the Preservation Society had been making drop-offs at my front door for weeks. Mrs. Friesen gave me a shoebox full of old letters that she'd translated from German and Mr. Wiebe found all these amazing black-and-white photos of early-twentieth-century Edenfeld's Main Street taken from the top of the feed mill. This, coupled with what I had derived from the dozens of family history books I'd ghostwritten, meant I'd actually written over a hundred pages by this point.

This year, the Golden Slumbers book sale was in the common room rather than the chapel. We weren't sure how to get past the front door, but thankfully the entrance-way was filled with old men sitting on wooden stools waiting for rides, always eager to let in strange young people who didn't look like murderers.

"Visiting your grandmother?" one man asked.

"No, just books," Katie said.

"What?"

"Books. We're here for the books."

He smiled and told us they were also selling some pretty nice toy tractors.

A poster on the wall advertised an upcoming screening of *The Sound of Music*.

"Hey, look, we should stick around for that," Katie joked. "I'll run home for some popcorn."

It's a popular movie around here because it promotes the idea of having large families and abandoning Catholicism. We also like *Fiddler on the Roof* because the one guy sings a lot about tradition.

I turned back to the old men sitting there.

"So, where's the book sale?" I asked.

"We're here for the book sale," Katie said, a little louder.

Then she noticed a handwritten note taped to the door that said, *Book Sale. Buzz: 3113.* She tried it. Someone answered, but there was so much static we couldn't make out what they were saying. A moment later, though, there was a loud buzzing noise and the door slowly opened on its own. The buzzing noise lasted far longer than was necessary. I tried to pull the door shut behind me, but it didn't budge.

"No need to force it," said one of the entranceway men. "It'll close all on its own. All in good time there, *jung*."

"Thanks."

I wiped my feet on the carpet. Katie took her shoes right off and placed them in a plastic bag to carry them. We were instantly hit with the aroma of cleaning supplies and body odour. A woman passed by. She looked like a nurse.

"Which way to the book sale?" Katie asked.

She said nothing, but pointed to another sign on the wall, which told us to refrain from drinking, smoking, or swearing and to continue to the end of the corridor.

We wandered down the dark hall, noticing that both the ceiling and carpet were stained. I heard an accordion being played, rather poorly, I'm sad to say, somewhere in the building. We found the room, which was the only one with an open door and the lights on. As soon as we entered, a woman with her hair in curlers handed us each a cardboard box and said it would cost us only ten dollars to fill it up with Harlequin romances. "You can take as much as you want." We took the boxes with us to be polite, even though it was unlikely we'd be hauling away that volume of steamy romance novels.

We made our way past the toy tractors and doilies and probably twenty tables of bonnet rippers to where the good books—my kind of books—were. It was disappointingly modest. Maybe three or four tables. They had none of the Toews classics. No Brandts or Janzens or Bergens, either. Not even any of the Wiebes. It was odd. I mean, I guess it was possible that it was just an off year. Maybe fewer people had died, leaving fewer personal libraries to be disposed of, but that seemed unlikely.

It didn't surprise me, however, to find Mrs. Friesen

and Mrs. Ens examining the selection. The way those two cruised through books, they were always in need of fresh used reading material.

"Pretty thin selection this year," Mrs. Friesen said.

"I've read more or less everything here," said Mrs. Ens.

They raised the possibility that maybe Mr. Wiebe had been here already and bought all the interesting books. He was on good terms with the nurses and also the men who sit near the entranceway and it was not impossible to think he might have been able to get in early.

"Just like you do, Sarah, at the garage sales," said Mrs. Ens.

I told them I was making good progress on the Edenfeld book and they said they were looking forward to reading it. In the end, the substandard selection didn't prevent each of them from leaving with half a dozen books under their arms.

I wasn't able to find much of interest myself, though I did find one of Randall's books. *Everything You Wanted to Know* ▮▮▮▮▮▮▮▮▮▮▮▮▮▮▮▮▮▮▮▮. It had been censored and I thought the new title gave a slightly wrong impression, not to mention that the censorship was completely unnecessary. The book is mostly just tips on the art of seduction, such as how to "sausage your way" into anyone's heart, or the swiftest way to remove your love interest's suspenders.

Katie was over in the Inspirational Literature section doing some shopping of her own. When I wandered over to join her, however, I noticed a copy of Elsie Dyck's *Scandalous Quotations* in her hands.

"You found that here?" I asked.

"No," Katie said. "I brought it along."

"Why would you bring a book to a book sale?"

She looked over her shoulder.

"This is why."

She wedged the book between *Stories of the Famous Hymns* and a well-worn cookbook called *1001 Ammonia Recipes*.

"I've brought some others," she said, rummaging through her purse. "See, look." She showed me the cover of *A Doll's Housebarn*.

I looked around. All we needed were mysterious men wearing sunglasses in lawn chairs watching this.

"They've got plenty of books here," Katie said. "No one will notice if I plant a few. I've penciled in five cents on the first page so somebody will buy them. These books might change lives."

She handed me an early work by Elsie Dyck called *Pilgrim at Edenfeld Creek* and said I should try it myself, saying it was just like planting a tree, but I was reluctant to even touch the thing.

"I can't, Katie. You know that."

She said I was being silly and shoved the book into my hands. Then she dragged me over to a stack of adult Sunday school material and guided me through the actions.

"It's easy. No one's even looking," she said.

I looked down at the book, Elsie Dyck's photo staring back at me. She had a perm in those days—maybe she still does—and a pleasantly wicked smile, as if goading me on. "You can do it, Timothy," I imagined her saying. "Just slide that book right in between those Bible commentaries over there." I thought about it. I even eyed a good spot, right in between the Chuck Swindoll and Warren Wiersbe. "No one will see you, Timothy. Just do it." There was enough space, I thought, right there, for Elsie.

Then a nurse went by, or an old man in a walker, I'm really not sure, but I was flooded with thoughts about my job and about people seeing me and about being associated with such things, and I couldn't do it. I gave the book back to Katie and apologized. I looked to the sky and whispered an apology to Elsie Dyck too.

"I'm sorry, Elsie. I don't know what's wrong with me."

"What are you doing?" Katie said. "She isn't dead."

"Well, not that we know of," I said.

Katie said I was being ridiculous and that she'd do the rest herself. She also said it was about time I went off to find Randall. I was just as disgusted with myself as Katie was.

I met Randall in the Russian Nonfiction section. Actually, he was on the edge of the Russia section, kind of infringing on Poland. I told him that was rather imperialist of him, but he didn't laugh. He takes Russia very seriously.

Evidently, he had been there a while, because he was cradling five copies of Mikhail Gorbachev's *Perestroika* in his arms. He gives them out as presents.

"I bought a few last year too," he said. "It's an important book."

"I'm sure it is."

"*Perestroika* means 'restructuring,'" Randall explained. "It was Gorbachev's last-ditch attempt to save the Soviet Union from collapsing by changing absolutely everything about it."

"No wonder the book is popular around here."

Edenfelders bought that book in droves. Their names, and often their addresses, were still inscribed on the front pages. *Peter Kauenhofen, 587 Koop Blvd. Grace Funk, #3-500 West Schroeder Road. Mrs. Helmut Fast, 1624 Peter Peters Lane, Edenfeld, Manitoba, R0A 2A0.* Evidently none of them had bothered to update their *ex libris* pages when BLT made us adopt all those California street names.

"I'm not just here for the Gorbachevs, though," Randall said. "I met someone."

"Oh, that's right. Well, I've been meaning to talk to you. I spoke with Brenda from Loans the other day and—"

"No, I mean I met someone online," he said. "That's why I need the dictionary. A Russian-English dictionary."

I had heard this from Randall before. He was always meeting women online, mostly after clicking on ads for some very suspicious websites. He once showed me a photo of this woman whose back was literally arched at a ninety-degree angle. I pointed out that it was physically impossible for a person to arch her back like that, but he said, "Even with a straight back she'd be an attractive woman." I don't think he understood what I was trying to say.

Katie found us. She was empty-handed, a sure sign of success. I had a hard time meeting her eyes.

"Now all we have to do is wait," Katie said.

"For what?" Randall asked.

"For the revolution."

Randall said he wasn't going to stick around for that and told Katie about the woman he met by clicking on an ad somewhere in the dark recesses of the Internet.

"She's smart and into books and speaks Russian," said Randall. "*Nyet*, *da*, the whole works!"

"So, she's not from Edenfeld, then?" Katie asked.

"No, no, of course not. You'd think I'd hook up with someone from Edenfeld?"

"Well, you haven't 'hooked up' with anyone yet," Katie said.

I tried to deflect Randall's error in judgment and move him back onto the straight and narrow path, or at least to the path that was less likely to have large sums of money withdrawn from his credit union account.

"Don't forget, there are plenty of women in Edenfeld too," I said. "You know, my cousin's single and there's also Brenda from Loans. Maybe you just need to be more assertive."

Katie rolled her eyes.

"I don't think you're anyone to lecture people about assertiveness," she said, then turned to Randall. "I think Brenda's into you, or haven't you noticed?"

"I'm not going to marry a Mennonite, Katie," he said.

Katie squeezed me close, replacing my lack of assertiveness with her own. I smiled.

"That's what we said too," Katie pointed out. She kissed me on the cheek.

It's true. We said it. We both thought we'd never marry a Mennonite. Thankfully we were both attracted to the sort of Mennonites who don't want to marry Mennonites so it cancelled out.

Randall was a hard man to convince, though.

"Russia's where our ancestors lived," he explained.

He hauled out an old atlas and pointed to some unlabelled area between two cities that had long since changed names. "This is where we lived. Well, the Hiebert side anyway."

"Yeah, for like fifteen minutes before the Makhnovists torched our villages and—"

"The Bolsheviks, you mean," Randall said.

Randall once did one of those DNA tests where you send them a sample of blood or a toenail or whatever and they send you back a piece of paper saying you're 17.3% Visigoth, or what have you. Randall was very disappointed to find out he was mostly northern European with a very small sprinkling of French. He disputed the results. "DNA does not a Russian make."

Sure, they call us "Russian Mennonites" because that's where we lived right before we came to Canada, but that's a misnomer. I mean, does Heppner sound Russian to you? How about Dyck or Vogt or Friesen? As far as I know, Russians have surnames like Rasputin and Smirnoff. Our ancestors lived for centuries in Prussia before relocating to the Russian Empire, and even then most of the colonies were in Ukraine, with only a handful in what is modern-day Russia and all those were way out in Siberia somewhere. Randall knows this stuff as well as I do, of course, but for some reason he's always been a Russophile. He once dressed as Baryshnikov for Halloween, a costume that got him promptly sent home from school with an angry note for his parents saying that students at our school "do not, under any circumstances, wear tights."

"Found one!" Randall said, pulling a dictionary from the pile and stacking it on top of his Gorbachevs.

"That's nice. So, you're going to learn Russian now?" I asked.

"I guess I'll need to if I'm going to pursue this relationship."

I stifled a laugh. I didn't want to rain on his parade, even if there was high probability this attractive, flexible Russian woman was actually a hairy, middle-aged man with flexibility no better than average. He showed me the picture on his phone.

"She looks nice," I said. "Where does she live?"

Randall told me the name. It was someplace in Russia, not one of the big cities, though. Not Moscow or St. Petersburg. Someplace small. Someplace that wasn't easy to research, I supposed.

I wanted to tell him to be careful. I wanted to say, "Hey Randall, get ahold of yourself!" I wanted to tell him to focus on his ghostwriting, maybe go home and brew some beer, or go out with a local woman who works at a credit union or something. That's what I wanted to say. Instead, I said, "You have my blessing, Randall," like I was a parent reluctantly consenting to allow my daughter to marry the Teichroeb boy from Gnadenheim.

Randall went home with five copies of *Perestroika*, three Russian-English dictionaries, and a thick green atlas of all the villages where our people used to live in the old country. He said he already had that atlas, but the copy he owned was in poor shape. He told me he had big plans.

I told Randall I'd treat him to a few Gorbachevs and brought the books to the payment table they had set up. Katie whispered that perhaps we didn't have the funds to feed Randall's Gorbachev habit, but I said Gorbachevs from Golden Slumbers were about the cheapest fix you could get. The woman with the cash box took her time, carefully opening each book to see the price pencilled in on the first page.

"That'll be two dollars and thirty-five cents," she said. "You didn't even fill a box."

She glanced over at Katie who handed in her box completely empty.

"Couldn't find anything you liked?" she asked.

"I'm not much of a reader," Katie said.

Randall said his goodbyes and carted off his haul. He wanted to get home and start brushing up on his Russian. He even said it that way too. "I've got to brush up," he said. Of course, he knew no Russian at all, not beyond the few words that everyone knows, but Randall's always overestimating his abilities. It's one of the things I like about him. I'm always preparing myself for failure. But Randall? Well, despite his criticisms of Edenfeld, I think one of the reasons he's stuck around so long is that he is somebody here. He's a writer. He's BLT's seconder. Now it seems he's also Edenfeld's foremost expert on the Russian language. He became our foremost expert the moment he bought that dictionary.

Katie and I didn't stay for *The Sound of Music*. I assumed the movie was for residents only and told her I had to get home and work on my book. She had a thesis to write too, I mentioned.

"I just want to stay a bit longer," Katie confessed. "See if anyone picks up those Elsie Dyck books."

I said that a criminal never sticks around at the scene of the crime. She didn't like me comparing her actions to criminal behaviour and said she thought of herself as a freedom fighter.

"I really need to get home and do some writing," I said. I wanted to get past page two hundred, which was a realistic goal for the evening, provided I didn't get distracted thinking about Randall's Gorbachevs and that atlas he got and the unsettling way he talked about his romantic plans.

My word count had been rising rapidly in the last few weeks and Katie wondered how on earth I had so much to say about such a small town. I said it wasn't the size of a town that mattered but the quality of its people. It was a quote I'd read on a billboard somewhere.

Katie said fine and that we could come back another day and sing "The Hills are Alive" with the seniors.

"I think they play that film every Friday."

When we got home, we were greeted with yet another fresh ice cream pail of muffins from Mrs. Janzen on our front step. At least, that's what I thought from a distance. When I got closer, however, I saw that it was actually a plastic bag hanging from the door handle and likely not from Mrs. Janzen at all. Inside, there was a very dodgy-looking loaf of bread—hard as a rock—and an unsigned note that said, *I know what you're baking.*

I read it again, slowly this time, my hands shaking.

"What on earth is this?" I asked, passing it to Katie.

Katie wasn't sure.

"A threat?" she wondered, then examined the bread closely and decided, unfortunately, that it was not edible.

"Better than a horse's head," she said, and went inside, leaving me standing there with loaf in hand. "Aren't you coming?"

I stood as still as that rock-hard bread while Katie

leaned against the door frame with a hand on her hip, then reached out and dragged me into the house.

"It's just a loaf of bread, Timothy," she said. "Come on now, don't you have some writing to do?"

She opened my laptop and plopped me down on the couch beside a pile of unread historic documents. Then she grabbed her own computer and scooched up beside me, ready to write.

I couldn't even move my fingers. The baking in this town was usually of such consistently high quality that a dried out *bultje* in a plastic bag could be perceived as nothing less than a threat. Katie hugged me around the waist and told me not to worry.

"We can dip it in our coffee in the morning," Katie said. I let out a deep breath. Then she intertwined her fingers in mine and placed my hands on the keyboard.

# Nine

I guess the perps figured one stale loaf of bread and a vague note would do for a while, because our doorstep was left undisturbed after that. The very next morning, Katie tossed the note in the trash and laughed at my suggestion that the police might want to dust it for prints. And, to be honest, although the stale loaf was always in the back of my mind, it didn't stop me from writing, though every sound—from birds striking the window to bored young dads doing donuts on Main Street parking lots—sent me rushing to my front steps to see if there'd been another deposit. I kept on writing, though. The Preservation Society was expecting a lot from me and I didn't want to let them down.

Soon, however, I discovered that Mr. Harder hadn't stopped writing either. I guess he hadn't received the doorstep loaf like I had. In the three months since he'd fired me, it seemed that he'd somehow miraculously completed his book without my help. Mrs. Ens told me she'd seen him struggling to operate the personal computer printers at the library.

"Get ready," she said. "I think he's about to launch."

Sure enough, within a few days, there were posters all over town displaying the cover his grandson Elmer had designed: a black-and-white photograph of Mr. Harder as a child on the farm, tilted sideways and bordered like a postage stamp. In large capital letters the poster read:

THE HARDER THEY FALL
*a book by*
DIETRICH F. HARDER

He had changed the title. There was no mention of my name.

I saw from the posters that the book launch was at five in the afternoon just after my leaf-blowing shift with Parks and Rec, exactly the time Mr. Harder and I used to meet at Ernie's. I thought it was rather considerate of him to schedule it at such a time when I would be able to attend, and I wondered if that was intentional. Maybe it was an olive branch of sorts. If it was his way of reaching out, then I decided I'd reciprocate and show up. My intentions weren't entirely reconciliatory, however, as the cheque he had given me had not, in fact, covered all my expenses and he still owed me a bit of cash.

When I arrived at Ernie's, I saw that they hadn't finished setting up all the chairs. I offered to help, but

Ernie said the arrangement of chairs required special training.

"Timothy, stand over there with your wife, yet," he said.

I replied, "Okay, sure, sounds good," but Katie had stayed at home to work on her thesis. I don't ask her to come to things like this.

I stood against the back wall and watched Ernie's specially trained individuals set up chairs and flirt. I wondered whether the flirting was part of the training or just an added benefit of the job. There was tape on the floor that indicated where the chairs should go and I thought that Ernie had vastly overestimated the difficulty of the task. Mr. Harder was there in the front row next to his wife, Justina, who was offering him a whole host of useful items, like moist towelettes and soda crackers, from deep inside her purse. I figured I'd wait until this whole thing was over to ask for my money.

At exactly quarter after five, Ernie went to the front and introduced Mr. Harder to the audience, recounting how they'd known each other since their time in the one-room schoolhouse in Hochstadt and how excited he was to see this newest Harder story finally brought to life. Seventeen people had showed up and that included me, Mr. Harder, Justina, and all six members of the set-up crew. City Sheila was there too, hawking her mascara. So it was a pretty good turnout, though I wasn't sure how he was ever going to sell all the copies he'd printed, even accounting for each of his grandchildren getting one at Christmas and maybe another one as a birthday gift or to pass along to a friend.

There wasn't much in the way of festivities. No reading. Not even a prayer of blessing meant to encourage book sales. I glanced about the room, looked at each and every person there, wondering if it was one of them who'd left the stale bread on my doorstep, but they were all busy chatting and drinking coffee and none of them looked any more suspicious or nervous than Edenfelders usually do in public places. All in all, the event was pretty casual. It was just a book-signing, really.

After everyone else had left, Mr. Toews, another former client, and Mr. Harder stood by the table of unsold books and spoke for a while in Plautdietsch interspersed with some English and a few words in regular German that we don't have in our version of the language. I took it from the tone, volume, and speed of their discussion that they were both quite happy with the book launch. I didn't want to interrupt their lovely repartee, but it was fairly urgent that I get that last payment from Mr. Harder. I was apprehensive, though, because there was always the chance Mr. Harder would say, "What last payment?" and then I wouldn't know whether he sincerely didn't remember or if he was just trying to save a few bucks.

"Oh, Timothy, yes, yes," Mr. Harder said. "Thanks for coming. I didn't forget you. Sorry to keep you waiting."

He reached into the metal box where he put all the money from his book sales.

"And here you are," he said. "Your cut."

I turned my back to him and counted the money. It was thirty-six dollars, most of it in rolls of quarters. I looked at Mr. Harder.

"This isn't how it works," I said.

"I understand, but I'll pay you the rest when I sell all my

books," he said. Then he asked me if I knew how he could get his book into the Dick Plett Library.

I couldn't believe it. Thankfully, I didn't have to explain.

"*Oba*, Harder! *Waut es met die!*"

Mr. Toews's tone had changed dramatically. I didn't understand much of what he was saying, but it was decidedly less chummy. He tried to explain things to Mr. Harder, switching to English for my benefit. There was no way he'd have gotten his three volumes completed, Mr. Toews said, if he wasn't paying his ghostwriter. You always have to pay your ghostwriter. After being properly scolded, Mr. Harder sheepishly pulled out his chequebook and paid me in full.

"I don't want Mr. Harder here ruining it for the rest of us," said Mr. Toews.

"Thank you. It's no problem," I said.

I pulled Mr. Toews aside for a moment. I wanted to know if maybe he needed some ghostwriting work done. I was running out of clients. I told him I might be able to squeeze him into my tight schedule.

"I'm afraid I don't have any new projects," he said, then lowered his voice. "I got the note."

"What?"

"The note. The order. Along with a basket of stale cupcakes," he said. "I've been shut down, I'm afraid."

"Shut down? By who?"

He shook his head.

"Don't be so naïve."

He explained that the only reason Mr. Harder had been allowed to publish his book was because it was so bowdlerized that it didn't mention a single word about Edenfeld.

"Have you seen it?" Mr. Toews said, urging me to open my copy. "It's basically nothing but photos of the Great Oak."

Mr. Harder approached and saw us flipping through the book.

"I think it turned out pretty well considering the circumstances," he said. "You should see the photo on page two-seventeen. Got a great angle on that one."

Then he took the book, opened it to the title page, and signed it.

"To Timothy. Thanks for all your hard work on this project. I don't think I could have done it without you. God bless, Dietrich F. Harder," he recited as he wrote.

But he *had* done it without me. Most of it, anyway. And as terrible as the end product was, it was his own, of sorts. It was his book, with his name on it, with his blurry photos and comma splices. I wondered how BLT managed to persuade him to take out all the stuff about his brother in the Conscientious Objector camp.

I wrote at a feverish pace after that, compelled, I suppose, by a strange combination of fear for my own livelihood and the desire to somehow undo the damage that had been done to Mr. Harder's life story. I looked through all the stuff I'd been given from Mr. Wiebe and Mrs. Friesen and pieced it together with large quantities of material from the Harder book and the Thiessen book and the Dueck book and the Bergen book and the Peters book and all the others I had written. When I reached four hundred pages, I was still only in the 1910s, just about the time when Prime Minister Robert Borden banned Mennonites from entering the country because our failure

to adequately assimilate into mainstream Canadian society was a grave threat to democracy or something. I think
Robert Borden and BLT Wiens would have been good
pals. They'd have probably opened a strip mall together:

*BORDEN AND WIENS SHOPPERS PARADISE*
*NOW FEATURING*
*FREE PARKING AND COUPONS*
*FOR KRAFT DINNER AND INSTANT COFFEE*
*TUCKED UNDER EVERY WIPER BLADE*

I had a century's worth of history yet to record, but I
was satisfied with my progress. The problem was not a
lack of material, but that I couldn't leave anything out.
All the stories that Mr. Harder was forced to cut, I wanted
to include. Whatever tales Mr. Toews wanted to get out
into the world were, to me, essential. Every time I even
thought about removing a story about Mrs. Dueck's apple
orchard or Mr. Letkeman's inaugural hymn sing, it felt like
I was tearing down a heritage building. So instead I kept
everything and the page count continued to grow like the
unraked leaves on our yard.

A few days after the Harder launch, Katie and I decided
to head over to the archives in Altfeld. If there was more
material out there to be had, I wanted to include it, and if
this meant the book was so thick that we needed to divide
it into two volumes or charge an extra dollar or two then
so be it.

Katie and I had been to the archives in Altfeld before,
or driven past it anyway. It was in this old stone building
on the edge of the village that used to hold the *Waisenamt*.

I heard that decades ago, some prudent members of the Preservation Society managed to squirrel away many of Edenfeld's most important historic documents at the regional archives in Altfeld. This was after they found out BLT was demanding that town secretaries destroy any records thirty years or older. "That's when the tax records expire," he had said. To my knowledge, pictures of deceased Edenfelders and pencil sketches of old homesteads have absolutely nothing to do with taxes, but BLT claimed he read it somewhere.

The archives weren't open yet when we arrived, so we sat in the truck and listened to classic rock on one of the city stations while a teenage boy fixed our stone chip. Occasionally, when the weather is right, you can pick up the rock station in Altfeld, but the signal's usually not very clear, and I've never liked the sound of the Doobie Brothers through the static. After a while, a man with a bow tie pulled up to the building on one of those antique high-wheel bicycles and unlocked the door for us. I asked him how that thing handled on the gravel roads and he referred me to Buster Keaton, which was a reference I didn't comprehend.

He reached out his hand and introduced himself.

"I'm Timothy," he said.

When I realized he wasn't kidding, I told him that was my name too, and Katie thought we'd better come up with some nicknames so there'd be no confusion. Katie suggested "Archives Timothy" but he said he was already well known in his circles as "Old Stuff Timothy" and would prefer to keep it at that. My name, Katie said, would simply be "Skinny Jeans Timothy," for obvious reasons. All this talk of Timothys seemed to ignite something in our guide because he rushed to the back room and retrieved the files of yet another Timothy. Timotheus Suderman, born 1829. "The first Mennonite ever to use that name," he said. Apparently, this original Timothy was quite the rebel for a nineteenth-century Mennonite. He had heard about the new world, had even been to California during the gold rush, but when it was time to find a wife, he buried his dreams, moved back to Russia, and married one of the Ewert sisters from the Ignatyevo colony. Old Stuff Timothy showed us a black-and-white photo of the Suderman family, years later, posing in front of an open casket at the patriarch's funeral. They were surrounded by horses.

"If only he had lived up to the promise of his name," Old Stuff Timothy said. "You know, if you're the only Timothy in a village of Jakobs and Johans, it's got to have some kind of impact. It singles you out."

"Like 'A Boy Named Sue,'" Katie said.

"Exactly."

Old Stuff Timothy led us to his office where he typed a few words into his computer, which still had a clunky old monitor and a floppy drive.

"I assume you've come here for your genealogy. That's what most people come here for. I can even tell you if you're related," he said, then pointed at Katie. "The two of you, we can see if you're *frindschauft*."

"Ummm, no thanks," I said.

But Katie perked up.

"I think this would be valuable information," she said. "Let's see the results."

I really didn't want to know. When it comes to information about how closely you are related to your wife, I think ignorance is bliss, but Katie said she was curious and it would be harmless and Old Stuff Timothy said the whole procedure was more-or-less painless.

"Do I have to pee into a cup or something?" I asked.

"No, no, no. Nothing like that. I just need your name and a birthdate," he explained. "For both of you."

According to Old Stuff Timothy, all he had to do was type "Timothy Heppner" and "Katie Brandt" into some genealogy software and within a few seconds it would churn out the myriad ways in which we are related. And related Katie and I are, in more than thirty different ways. Fourth cousins once removed. Fifth cousins. Fifth cousins once removed. Sixth cousins. Sixth cousins twice removed. Seventh cousins. Seventh cousins once removed. It kept going.

"It doesn't go back further than the 16th century," he said. "Otherwise we'd find more connections."

"Well, that's a relief."

Katie eagerly took the fifteen-page document and tucked it into her purse. She said she was going to pin it above our queen-size bed. I cringed at the thought.

"Fourth cousins is no big deal," she said. "So we share one common ancestor born sometime in the 1700s. Who cares? We're all related if you go back far enough."

"It's true," said Old Stuff Timothy. "You know, years ago a Sunday school teacher once told me that Adam and Eve's children must have married their own brothers and sisters. Being married to your cousin isn't so bad. It's biblical."

I told both Katie and Old Stuff Timothy that we

absolutely were not here to obtain our genealogical records and that I'd prefer if we didn't discuss it any further. They kept going, however, I think because they could see it was making me uncomfortable. Finally, I stood in front of them.

"Got anything about Edenfeld history?" I asked.

Old Stuff Timothy became serious. Without a word he walked over to the door and locked it. He made us put on white gloves, even though we'd already promised not to touch anything, then he disappeared behind a curtain. Katie nudged me to follow.

"It's okay, you can come back here," he said.

He slid down a narrow aisle that he could barely fit through, and Katie and I had equal difficulty, especially since I insisted on walking astride her and holding her hand the whole way down the aisle.

"From here," he said, pointing way above his head, "to there at the end by the wall."

I scanned to the back of the room. There were dozens of boxes, maybe over a hundred, all indexed and numbered and piled high on the shelves. I noted the sprinklers on the ceiling.

"All of this is about Edenfeld?" I asked.

"Yeah, I'm glad we were able to save it," he said.

"Save it from what?"

Old Stuff Timothy looked at me like that was the most inane question he'd ever heard.

I took a deep breath. This was a lot to go through. More than I could handle. I didn't know how I could possibly include it all. I peeked into a box near me and flipped through the contents. Photos. A few old letters. A ledger from a store that no longer existed. Then I slid it back into place and handed Katie the keys.

"Is it okay if we back it up onto the yard?"

"Back what up?" Old Stuff Timothy asked.

"The truck," I said.

He laughed.

"This is an archive, sir," he said. "I can't let you take anything from the building, but you're more than welcome to look around. We close at six. You can also make copies if you want."

Katie told Old Stuff Timothy that, of course, I knew all this already and that I had only been kidding about the truck. She pocketed the keys.

We thanked Old Stuff Timothy and I told him I'd come back again to explore more thoroughly. He said I could come back whenever I wanted, but it was better if I called ahead since he didn't want to have to take his penny-farthing out on the gravel more than was necessary.

"It's rough on the tires," he said. "Especially the big front one."

I promised I'd call and waved goodbye.

Katie expertly navigated our way back home, including a really close call with a Massey Ferguson, but I was too distracted to care. I thought about the archives—all those boxes—and it dawned on me then that I might never finish the Edenfeld book, not if I had to go through everything. Not if I had to include everything. There was always more. And for a moment, the thought that I might never finish the book, the thought that it might never be published and that my name might never get out there, gave me a sense of relief.

That night, Katie pinned the genealogy to the headboard, looked amorously at me from between the sheets, and moved in closer to snuggle. I guess you know how things tend to go from there. Well, anyway, throughout the entire encounter, I couldn't help but think about the fact that she was my fourth cousin. "Once removed," she reminded me.

Afterwards, Katie got up, threw on a nightgown, and sat on the sofa, working on her thesis late into the night.

"You should get to work too," she said from the other room.

As I lay alone in bed, I thought about Mr. Harder's book launch and how proud he had been to sign his own name. Even if the thing wasn't much more than a bunch of old photos, he was, in a sense, a real writer. And me? I wanted to hide, avoid stale loaves of bread on the front porch, and just keep typing and typing, hoping they'd all just forget they'd even tasked me with the job in the first place. I didn't even want my name on the cover of this book I couldn't stop writing. "I'm just a ghostwriter," I'd told the Preservation Society at our last meeting. "You folks can take the credit." I remember Katie's reaction. She said my name should be on the cover in big, bold letters and to hell with BLT if he didn't like it. Mrs. Friesen replied that we were not to make any assumptions about BLT's eternal destiny, but, yes, perhaps it didn't matter what he thought.

Somewhere above me was the utterly embarrassing printout of all the ways Katie and I were cousins. More disturbing for me than the genealogy hanging over my head was the thought that I was the Timothy in a long line of Jakobs and Johans. Yes, I was the Timothy, and I was doing absolutely nothing to live up to my name.

# Ten

I think I'd consumed about four free hot dogs and two bags of plain chips by the time the mayor showed up to give his annual State of Edenfeld address in front of the town hall on Main Street. It was cold and cloudy, not ideal hot dog weather, but despite the risk of snow, BLT always waited until early November for this speech; he didn't like to compete with the credit union hot dog giveaways throughout the summer. After a month or two without free hot dogs, his early November giveaway always drew impressive crowds. There were probably a hundred people there. I was obligated to show up, but I didn't mind. I'd sit through any hour-long speech if it meant a free lunch.

"As soon as it's over," said Mr. Vogt, "there's some graffiti we've got to clean up." Someone had sprayed PROGRESS IS REGRESS in huge red letters on the back of one of

BLT's strip malls. Also CLASS OF 1965. I could think of a few suspects.

Katie once told me she thought BLT looked a bit like Edward G. Robinson, the actor from all those 1930s gangster films. "Only taller," she said. She showed me a picture and I agreed there was an uncanny resemblance, other than the height difference, of course, and the fact I'd never seen BLT Wiens, or any Edenfeld man for that matter, wear a fedora or smoke a cigar. I guess BLT's infectious Edward G. Robinson smile, his occasional nods to family values, and his megamart-based promises are what keeps him in power in this town. It certainly isn't his powers of elocution.

BLT stood on the steps of the town hall, one hand gripped firmly on the podium, so the wind wouldn't knock him over, and the other gripped firmly around a hot dog. There were two large spots of mustard on his tie.

"Friends, let me tell you a story," he began. "As you know, I have been your mayor for almost thirty years now. Those of you who are younger will not remember this, but anyone of a certain age will recall the old bridge that used to cross the creek by the water tower ..."

Then he launched into this rather tedious account of the summers he spent playing under the bridge and how he watched, year after year, as the structure deteriorated.

"The bridge is not there anymore. And do you know why that is? It washed away one summer and came ashore three days later behind the old Catholic church in Ste. Adèle. Poor workmanship from the Wohlgemuth boys. Thankfully, they moved to Altfeld decades ago. I'm sure you've all heard the story about the wise man who built his house on a rock, while the foolish man built his house on sand. When the rains came, which house do you think remained? The one built on a solid foundation. This, my friends, is exactly what I've been building in this great town of ours, with your help, of course."

His most enthusiastic fans were near the front and cheered him on between bites of hot dog. Less keen were the rest of us in the back, just there for the free food. I heard a few murmurs nearby about BLT's questionable interpretation of scripture.

There was a tap on my shoulder. It was Mrs. Friesen from the Preservation Society. Mr. Wiebe was there too.

"Mrs. Ens is quilting," she said. "She sends her regrets. You know how she is."

I knew from experience that these folks were not all that desirous of cheap, undercooked wieners.

"So you came to hear the mayor, eh?" I asked.

"Something like that," Mrs. Friesen said.

The sound guy turned up the volume. We ceased chatting and gave our attention to the man at the podium.

"Before my ascension to power, Edenfeld had suffered through decades of poor leadership. We were a house built on sand. It wouldn't be appropriate to mention any names, but I can't say that Mayor Gerbrandt and Mayor Banman did our town any favours. We had gravel roads. We had not a single fast food chain, nor the empty lots necessary to accommodate a big-box store—certainly not with sufficient room for parking. Just think of what visitors must have thought in those days, to drive into Edenfeld only to find horses on every block and families speaking Plautdietsch. How can we expect people to come and do business here if they can't even communicate with us? The situation was embarrassing and hardly fitting for a progressive community like ours. Too many mayors, for too many years, kept us stuck in a rut. In fact, there was a period of nearly four decades before I took office when not a single new parking lot or church gymnasium was built in this town. Yes, friends, before I was mayor, Edenfeld was in rough shape."

He finished the last bite of his hot dog and licked his fingers. The sound could be clearly heard in the microphone. I grimaced and almost felt bad for him. Then again, none of his supporters up front seemed to be fazed. He dried his fingers on a pant leg and then made a wild flailing motion that sent Mr. Vogt into action.

"Go on up there," Mr. Vogt said.

"What?"

"Yeah, you've got to go up there. Mr. Wiens is beckoning."

I wasn't sure what this was all about, but I was on the clock, so I passed my hot dog to Mr. Wiebe for safekeeping and pushed through the crowd.

"Excuse me, uh, sorry, I've got to go. I've got to go to the front apparently."

I looked back at Mrs. Friesen. She waved slowly and mouthed the words "good luck," which only made me even more uneasy.

Soon I was joined by a dozen other Parks and Rec employees, all wearing bright orange vests and hard hats that we held in front of us like we were preparing for a penalty kick. A couple Thiessen boys had forgotten their headgear and Mr. Vogt ushered them back off the stage saying it was "giving the wrong impression about our commitment to safety." Sweat ran from my brow, but I just let it trickle down and slide off the bottom of my chin. I took a deep breath. BLT turned around and looked straight at me, or so it seemed. He scanned his line of employees, shook the hand of the person closest to him, and faced the audience once more.

"Today is a great day for our community," he said.

Then, in a much more official entrance, a parade of men in out-of-date and ill-fitting business suits marched onto the stage in front of us. Music—some horrible pop song with thumping bass—played from a sound system rented for the occasion. These were the town councillors. Most of them were also elders at the Faith Barn. The only exceptions were Dr. Dryden, a nominal Anglican who had moved to Edenfeld a decade ago to open a clinic and who BLT had immediately appointed head of the town Englishification Committee, and Mr. Pankratz, a South Edenfeld member who, at nearly ninety years of age, had been left on the board to appease his fans from his days as goaltender for the 1947 Bergthal Cup champions, the Edenfeld Saints. He always wore his old hockey jersey at events like this. They squeezed in front of us. Parks and Rec backed up. There wasn't much room left on the stage.

The crowd gave us all a warm welcome. I should be precise: about nine or ten people clapped, and one woman attempted, but failed, to whistle with her fingers, but that was as much enthusiasm as I had heard in Edenfeld in quite some time.

"Before I was mayor," BLT continued, "progress was considered a dirty word around here."

Just then, a clenched fist emerged defiantly above the sea of heads.

"It is!" yelled Mrs. Friesen.

Mr. Wiebe held up a carboard sign that read:

PRESERVE OUR HERITAGE BUILDINGS!

"Save the Elsie Dyck house!" yelled Mrs. Friesen.

This wasn't good. As they moved forward, the crowd gave way and I looked down and silently prayed they would not involve me in any of this. Soon they were right up at the front in amongst all the die-hard BLTers who put hot dogs in their mouths and kept their distance, not wanting to be associated with the protest.

"As I was saying," continued BLT, "progress used to be considered a dirty word around here."

"No progress at the expense of our heritage!" yelled Mrs. Friesen.

"I see that some unfortunate souls still think it is," said BLT. "Well, let me tell you, I am not threatened by a few individuals with their heads stuck in the slop bucket of life. I am sick and tired of feeding from that bucket, as I'm sure you all are too. If these regressives don't like our town, as far as I'm concerned, they can leave on the next train … and once we have the track built it will be much easier for them to do so."

A man from the audience began chanting "build that track, build that track," but it didn't catch on.

BLT stepped back as if to adjust his balance, and so did his councillors. I had no choice but to hop off the back of the stage, where I stood with my face squarely in the back of Mr. Bueckert's sweaty, checkered 1980s suit jacket. It was like staring into the abyss.

I couldn't see a thing, but heard a raucous round of applause. Then I heard yelling, a woman scream, some clapping, a collective gasp, and moments later, Mr. Vogt was breathing down my neck.

"Get out there, now!"

"What?"

"You know them. They'll listen to you."

He pulled me around the stage and into the crowd. By that time, a few orange-vested members of the Parks and Rec crew had surrounded Mrs. Friesen and Mr. Wiebe and shoved them off to the side like the rubble of a house-barn. I stared at Mrs. Friesen and turned to look at Mr. Wiebe. Mr. Vogt urged me to proceed.

"Why don't you just go?" I said. "It would be better if you just left."

One of the Thiessen boys stepped closer.

"Don't touch them," I said. "They'll leave."

Mr. Wiebe handed me my hot dog. He hadn't even taken a bite.

As they departed, the crowd made room like the parting of the Red Sea. Mrs. Friesen shouted something, Mr. Wiebe held his sign in the air, and I stood there like a fool, ashamed of myself. Some people cheered, although it wasn't entirely clear who was cheering in solidarity and who was cheering at their departure.

"Now that that unpleasantness is behind us..." BLT continued.

There were a few boos, not many mind you, but enough that BLT looked uncomfortable and Mr. Vogt ushered us back into our positions and once again I was crammed behind Mr. Bueckert. I could see BLT raise his arms—I saw them peak above the heads of the men in front of me—and direct our attention to a large, covered object that was being wheeled in next to the stage. He motioned for the music to start up again, then stepped away from the podium, sidled up beside whatever it was, and gripped the rope that was dangling there. He paused for moment, waiting for the music to reach a crescendo, then swiftly pulled back the curtain.

"Behold, a new name for a new town," he said. "I give you, Pretty Plain!"

A chunk of hot dog flew from my mouth.

A gaudy metal sign loomed next to me with the words:

WELCOME TO PRETTY PLAIN
POPULATION 4,512
*… and counting!*

The population number was digital, presumably so that BLT could bump the numbers in an upward direction right before an election. Below the words was an aerial photograph of a generic suburb in Arizona or somewhere and a stock photo of a smiling nuclear family. The woman in the picture was pregnant and the man was rubbing her belly while two other children climbed on his shoulders. They were all wearing matching denim jeans and polo shirts, and every one of them had bleach-blonde hair and perfect white teeth. BLT explained this new sign would be replacing the "old, boring, German one" later in the week. And even better, BLT said, they were going to twin the highway to the city.

"With your help and a few loads of concrete, Pretty Plain will become a glorious new bedroom community for the city. We will welcome the world!"

A few people clapped, but this time the whistling woman didn't even attempt it.

I stood there, wedged behind the town council, and peered at the sign. I noticed then that I was standing close to an electrical cable, one that, with just an accidental tug, might turn out the lights on this whole operation. I inched over slowly and stepped right on the cord, then peeked around Mr. Bueckert.

"Oh, careful there, Timothy. You don't want to trip."

It was Mr. Vogt.

"Time to get back to work. There's some graffiti that needs cleaning ..."

"Right," I said. "The graffiti."

I looked at the flashy new sign. The population number had gone up by half a dozen people.

So the town was getting a new sign. More importantly, a new name. As we walked to the truck, Mr. Vogt handed us Velcro patches to put on our orange vests that read, *Town of Pretty Plain, Manitoba*. These were to go over the existing ones, a temporary measure until the replacement vests arrived. Then we went to the strip mall to remove the graffiti.

For the next few days, the new name was the talk of the town, or at least the talk of the diner above the gas station.

"It's no big deal," I heard one man say. "Edenfeld is not the first town around here to make a name change."

This is true. A decade ago there was a real push to turn our villages into commuter towns and so Schlammfeld became Newtown and Untersumpfdorf became Fairview. Until now, Edenfeld had always avoided such a fate because enough people thought the term "bedroom community" was too suggestive.

"*Oba*, if we want to have the Englishers come here yet, then we need to have a sign for the Englishers, so they'll know that we want them to come here yet, despite the fact they're Englishers. They can come yet, the Englishers."

The conversations at Ernie's got pretty heated. I saw one man push the menu he was holding into a second man's chest and the second man stood up and said he wasn't going to be having breakfast with the first one anymore. There's nothing more detrimental to a relationship around here than to cancel a long-standing breakfast date. Such arrangements usually last until one of the breakfasters dies or moves to Golden Slumbers where all the meals are provided.

Later that week, the Pretty Plain sign went up. They also put another one way out on the highway to promote the new name. It claims Pretty Plain is only forty minutes from the city. However, you have to drive far out into the country to reach the sign, and then, after that, you have to drive well above the speed limit to reach the outskirts of Pretty Plain in under an hour. The sign was facing incoming, not outgoing, traffic, and when Randall saw it, he said he thought it would make a lot more sense if they turned it around.

I really didn't want to attend the next Preservation Society meeting. I didn't know how I was going to face Mr. Wiebe and Mrs. Friesen. Just before we should have been leaving for the meeting, I told Katie it was too bad, but I needed to stay back this time and do some yardwork. Katie said that I never volunteered to do yardwork and that there really wasn't much of it to do at this time of year anyway. I took her outside, turned on the light that lit up the backyard, and pointed out the leaves, saying there was a new batch to clean up every day, it seemed.

"What's going on?" she asked.

I said nothing was going on and grabbed the rake. She told me she was going to go to the meeting without me, and that people would ask where I was and that she was going to tell them the truth. "He didn't want to come."

I thought about just letting her go. I even started to make a mound of soggy leaves, but when I saw through the window that she'd already put on her coat and was heading for the front door, I dropped the rake and rushed back inside to stop her.

"Don't go," I said. "You'll hate me ..."

"And why is that?" she wanted to know.

I sat her down on the sofa and tried to think of how I was going to present my actions at BLT's speech in as positive a light as possible. She gripped my hands firmly, like I was about to take a polygraph.

"Mr. Wiebe and Mrs. Friesen were there," I said. "They were protesting ..."

I paused for a long while, Katie looking intently at me, squeezing tight.

"I really didn't want to side with the mayor, but I didn't have a choice ..."

I told her I was on the clock, that I was wearing an orange vest, and there was nothing else I could do. I think

I even tried to say that it was probably for their own good, but if I said it, I didn't mean it.

"I'm sorry," I said.

Katie kept silent and when I tried to go in for a hug, she backed off and told me in rather colourful language that I could go sleep with one of my other fourth cousins that night. Then she stood up in the dark room, looking straight down at me.

"What are you going to do to make this right?" she said.

I told her I didn't know.

She said she had a lot of thinking to do, and so did I. Now, however, it was too late to go to the meeting, so Katie said she was going to drive out to look at the sign on the highway. Alone.

I waited there on the sofa sitting upright and stiff—I didn't move, didn't turn on the television, didn't even work on my book—and I was still in the same position when she arrived back home a couple hours later.

"Edenfeld is vanishing," Katie said, moving in close to see my face in the dim light.

I didn't say a word, but reached out and held her in my arms. That night we slept on the couch together.

# Winta

# Eleven

I imagine BLT was pretty happy that he managed to get in one last hot dog rally before the snow fell. We had our first winter storm right after, leaving only half the crew to change all the signs to the new town name while the rest of us cleared the streets of snow and dumped it all in an empty Main Street lot. For some reason, I'd been put on snow-clearing duty with the oldest Thiessen boy, who, at nearly thirty, was a boy in maturity level only. I was actually glad I wouldn't be forced to change the signs, but I did wonder why I'd been demoted to babysit Fart-Joke Thiessen. On top of that, we had to get up at four o'clock. Mr. Vogt always made us wake up extra early after a snowstorm because we had to get the streets cleared before the minivans and pickup trucks started rolling. I set my alarm for three thirty, kissed Katie without waking her, and threw on my winter clothes. The orange vest barely fit over my winter parka. I requested a larger one but Mr. Vogt said something about how I shouldn't complain and to instead think of all the starving children across the globe who don't have any orange vests, let alone nicely fitting ones.

So now there's a massive snow hill on one of the empty lots. The children sometimes sled down these Parks and Rec creations, but they're not supposed to. It's dangerous. Last year I almost buried one of the Doerksen kids, so this time we put up a sign. DANGER. NO SLEDDING. BY ORDER OF THE TOWN OF PRETTY PLAIN. It hasn't been much of a deterrent, though, so I had to get my assigned Thiessen to stop watching hunting videos on his phone and run out there to shoo away the children right before we dumped a load. Crushing dreams is just part of our job.

On my way home from work, I checked the mail and found a letter from the credit union. It was threatening and urgent and translated into three languages that I might plausibly know so there was no chance of any mis-communication. It seemed that ever since Randall had started cyber-dating his fictitious Russian sweetheart, Brenda from Loans had stopped telling her manager that our missed payments were accidental. Or maybe she'd just heard about my actions at BLT's speech. Either way, I still didn't have the money for the mortgage. In the end, Mrs. Esau's soup-based poetry book didn't pay much and I hadn't attracted any new clients since the summer.

I figured since I was at the post office anyway, I might as well check out the bulletin board and see how my ad was doing. I was also looking forward to reading the

Inspirational Verse of the Month, which took up prime real estate in the centre of the bulletin board. Sometimes, if the verse is particularly well received, they might even leave it up there for a few months in a row. All last winter it said: *Now take your son, your only son, Isaac, whom you love, and go into the land of Moriah. Offer him there as a burnt offering on one of the mountains which I will tell you of (Genesis 22:2)*. This time, however, there was no verse at all, just dozens of posters, which was peculiar since people don't usually have garage sales in the middle of November for fear of one of the Bickerts slipping and falling and having to convalesce in the seller's spare bedroom for the next six weeks. Eventually, I found my ad. It was partially covered by a glossy leaflet announcing the brand new "stain-free" carpets and improved strawberry daiquiris at the bar on Sunset Strip.

I wanted to move my ad to a better spot, but there wasn't much space. I thought of pinning it right into the wall. Maybe I could use Scotch Tape to avoid making a hole, but then that might peel the paint off when removed, so I didn't do that either. Instead, I just closed my eyes, reached up, tore a random paper from the board, and placed mine in its spot. Then I crumpled up my unlucky victim without looking and threw it in the trash. I didn't want to know whose livelihood I was disrupting.

I left the post office and walked past the Elsie Dyck house. I stopped there for a moment and looked at the FOR SALE sign. The price had been reduced, but evidently this had not attracted any buyers. I thought about the ad at the post office. Elsie never would have resorted to such tactics. Wracked with guilt, I went back, scrounged the ad from the trash bin, and replaced it in its spot. It was in a little worse shape, but it was legible. *Vereniki. $10 a dozen. Contact Margaret Waldner.*

By the end of the day, I was exhausted and desperately in need of a shower, but I didn't have time because there was an emergency meeting of the Preservation Society. Katie texted and said she was already there and that it would probably be a good idea if I showed up. I hoped my rather pathetic, unkempt appearance and mild pungency might sway them towards forgiveness. I was nervous, though, and having missed the last meeting only made my apprehensions worse.

The church was booked all week with funeral receptions and family gatherings, so we had to meet in Mrs. Friesen's living room. This change in locale meant we couldn't watch *The Earl Warkentin Story: Adventures of a Wandering Schekjbenjel.* Mrs. Friesen's VCR had stopped working ages ago and she'd never bothered to get it fixed. "I watch the Blue Bombers sometimes," she explained, "but otherwise I never even turn on the TV."

When I arrived, Mrs. Friesen greeted me with a firm handshake and handed me a glass of Malbec.

"One of the benefits of not meeting in the church basement," she said, guiding me down the hall to the living room.

Her walls were covered with pictures of her grandchildren and a few snapshots of a trip to Peru she'd taken with her late husband.

As we walked past Machu Picchu, I tried to explain my behaviour at the rally, about Mr. Vogt and BLT, and I think I said "I'm sorry" about half a dozen times before Mrs.

Friesen told me "enough is enough" and that she got the idea already. By this time we were standing right in the middle of the living room and the conversation around us ceased. They looked up at us.

"Listen, Timothy, we got out of that event exactly what we were hoping for," Mrs. Friesen said.

"You were hoping to be manhandled by Eddie Thiessen?" asked Brenda from Loans, who had a glass of white in one hand and a red in the other.

"No, I mean exposure. Publicity," said Mrs. Friesen. "I think we drew attention to some very important issues."

The presence of a new member at the meeting was cited as evidence of the protest's effectiveness.

"Hi, City Sheila," I said. "Nice to see you here."

Mrs. Friesen told me to sit down, but I said I'd prefer to stand.

"Fine," Mr. Wiebe said, "but then at least don't stand there in the middle of the room like you're about to confess your sins before the congregation."

Mr. Wiebe pointed out a perfect spot for me along the wall next to the dieffenbachia. Mrs. Friesen unnecessarily poured me some more wine. Then the meeting officially opened with the singing of an old hippie song they all seemed to know. It was something about a hammer and a bell and everyone living in peace and harmony.

"No need for a hymn, since we're not in a church," said Mrs. Friesen.

When we were finished singing, Mrs. Ens muttered that she'd never really liked that song because it sounded a bit "socialist" to her and she thought we had left all that garbage behind in the Soviet Union. Mr. Wiebe said the sweet

149

harmonies of Peter, Paul, and Mary were "fairly innocent in my books," and Mrs. Friesen mentioned that she'd been singing that song since the early sixties and never once did it inspire a radical redistribution of wealth. She pointed to a brand new broach on her blouse. Very pricey. Only then was Mrs. Ens satisfied that the group had not become corrupted too badly by Bolshevism.

The next point on the agenda was to reaffirm our commitment to never ever refer to Edenfeld as Pretty Plain. City Sheila said she hadn't lived in Edenfeld as long as the others, but agreed with everyone else that the new name was absolutely ridiculous, like putting lipstick on a pig. "Not that Edenfeld's a pig," she clarified.

They'd already made the pledge at the last meeting, but since Katie and I hadn't been there, Brenda from Loans suggested that we all spit into the palms of our hands and squeeze them together in a pact. Mr. Wiebe attempted it for a moment, but couldn't conjure up enough saliva and then Mrs. Friesen said she was worried her furniture might get water damage and everyone agreed we'd never use the name Pretty Plain and that a spit pact was probably not necessary.

"I don't speak German, not even Plautdietsch, and I think the name change is an utterly fatuous idea," said Katie.

She had to explain what "fatuous" meant and when we learned it meant she was against the name change, and had nothing whatsoever to do with the volume of baked goods we were enjoying, we all nodded our heads in agreement.

"If BLT's idea of progress means he wants to join me in rallying the citizenry to allow women to walk into a church meeting without their heads covered, I'm all for it," Katie continued, "but erasing history and changing names? I mean, I'm not sure Edenfeld will even be Edenfeld anymore by the time he's done with it."

I once read about how all the cells in your body are constantly dying and being replaced with new ones, to the degree that within a few years after birth you're actually an entirely different person at the molecular level. I mentioned this to the others, but they always give me a hard time whenever I get too philosophical, especially if my philosophy is incoherent or mediocre.

"Plus, your biology is all wrong," said Mr. Wiebe.

He used to teach science in the city and has gotten considerable flack in Edenfeld since he's "one of those people who believes the world is billions of years old and all that." I suppose after the highway's twinned, though, everyone around here will be reading books by Englishers and thinking their ancestors were monkeys, and I guess BLT will chalk that up as an unfortunate, unintended consequence of what otherwise was a marvelous plan to reinvent Edenfeld.

One thing was clear—the Edenfeld Preservation Society would remain the Edenfeld Preservation Society. No name change there.

"They can have their Pretty Plain Megamart and their Pretty Plain Dollar Store, but there's no way I'm ever going to be a part of anything called the Pretty Plain Preservation Society," said Katie.

I mentioned that BLT had added a tidy sum of money to the Parks and Rec budget to address any vandalism that might occur to the new sign and while I explained this,

Mrs. Friesen avoided looking at me and Mr. Wiebe called for the next item on the agenda.

Brenda from Loans stood up to give her report on the Elsie Dyck house, or rather, to showcase the new tattoo on her left ankle.

"Want to see my Zwingli?" she asked.

Curious, or perhaps confused, Mrs. Ens nodded and said, "Oh, sure, it's always good to check for Zwinglis."

And so there it was. Her new tattoo: Ulrich Zwingli. His black hat with the flaps over the ears reminded me of something the Thiessen boys wore when out ice fishing or checking the trapping lines, but I didn't want to mention the Parks and Rec crew yet again so I kept this comparison to myself. Plus, Zwingli probably didn't ice fish. Also, by then Mr. Wiebe was well into a lecture about the falling out that Zwingli had with Conrad Grebel and the time had long passed for me to make a pithy remark even if I had the desire.

"Anyway, I want to reassure everyone that the Elsie Dyck house is still on the market," Brenda from Loans said, "but it's an old house and if anyone even wanted to buy it, it would require a lot of repairs. The people who are moving here from the city want new houses, like those ones on the edge of town by the golf course. I'm sure the house will sell eventually, but for now it's sitting there empty. Even the renters have moved out."

"And the plaque? Any chance of that?" asked Mr. Wiebe.

"It doesn't look like we'll get any money for a plaque, I'm afraid, but there's still a chance we can raise the funds ourselves, maybe even enough to save the building, who knows."

Katie wondered just how many molasses cookies it would take to purchase a house like that. Mr. Wiebe got out his calculator and was still crunching the numbers long after Katie assured him she had been kidding.

Neither Katie nor I were all that keen on the financial efficacy of a bake sale. The annual Edenfeld Bake Sale and Flea Market was usually well attended, but we doubted the profits would be all that substantial unless we were selling mason jars. City Sheila said all proceeds from her makeup tutorials on the day of the bake sale would go to support the Elsie Dyck fund. It wouldn't be a lot of money, but if we didn't earn enough to buy the house, we might very well earn enough to at least put a plaque in front of it and, so far, the presence of plaques has kept at least a few buildings around here from being demolished.

"Plus, your book, Timothy," said Mr. Wiebe. "It's important."

I wished they would stop saying that. "I think you're overestimating the power of my—"

"It will remind people of our past and our heritage."

By this time, the Edenfeld book had ballooned to more than six hundred pages. It's true that many of those pages were filled with pictures and maps. Still, being the town saviour was a heavy burden and I reminded them that, technically speaking, it was not actually my book.

"It's a Preservation Society project," I said.

The whole conversation was making me sweat. I kept thinking about that unfriendly loaf of bread on my doorstep. I mean, I was already risking my livelihood by telling "the truth, the whole truth, and nothing but the truth" about Edenfeld's history, and now I was being asked to bake a few cookies laced with arsenic. Well, the arsenic part was brought up as a joke. Nevertheless, these would be dangerous cookies, as baking tends to be around here, and I don't just mean the sugar cookies Elsie Dyck supposedly undercooked all those years ago. No, I mean these cookies would be seen as a threat, perhaps one even more pointed than the stale bread on my porch. It didn't help that Mrs. Friesen had plans to write *Buildings of the Past. Values of the Future* in bright red icing and tiny, tiny printing on all her baked goods from now on.

I felt it was time to make my exit. I said I had some baking to do, and more writing, and, avoiding the disheartened look Katie was giving me, I left Mrs. Friesen's warm house to trudge through the snow over to Randall's, hoping he'd return the copy of the *Mennonite Treasury Cookbook* that I'd lent him a while back.

He told me to use the back door to avoid the neighbours. They'd been known to report suspicious activity before, like that time one spring when we burned five years of dead Christmas trees that Randall had been saving for the occasion. The flames were three metres high and we were worried they might reach the hydro lines and then the power would go out and the beer in the fridge would get warm. It didn't happen, though, thanks to Randall's quick thinking and easy access to the garden hose.

I found him sitting alone in his garage eating sunflower seeds. It appeared that he'd been there for a while because the pile of shells was rather substantial.

"I've been experimenting," he said.

"Experimenting?" I asked. "Like in real-life, in-person dating?"

He explained that he wanted to go through the entire *Mennonite Treasury Cookbook* and turn all those recipes into different types of beer. He even added some star anise to his latest concoction. "Star anise and Rogers Golden Syrup make a great IPA," he said, pouring me a glass. I didn't agree, but it was free, so I also didn't complain.

"So you can take the cookbook with you, but I need it back ASAP," he said.

He handed it to me like I was about to cook up some hash brownies.

"What exactly are you baking?"

"Oh, nothing. It's for a fundraiser."

"I see," he said. "For the ramp at the hospital, I assume."

"Done any seconding lately?" I asked.

"Oh, a few times. Here and there. You know how it is, Timothy."

"No, I don't."

"Been reading about Russia, Siberia," he said. He watched me paging through the cookbook. "I need that back, you know."

He said it like it was his book, not mine, but Randall tends to get that way. He's kind of possessive.

I agreed to get it back to him as soon as I made my required six dozen Grandma cookies. I wasn't a grandmother and had no intentions of ever being one, but Mrs. Ens had already signed up to make *tweeback* and Mr. Wiebe was going to make farmer sausage *schnetje* and Mrs. Friesen and Brenda from Loans were teaming up to make a cold plum soup that we call *plümemoos*. All this, coupled with City Sheila's ever-popular eyeliner lessons, meant that baking some Grandma cookies was the only option Katie and I had left.

"I broke up with Svetlana," Randall said.

"The flexible Russian?" I asked.

"Yeah," he said. "It wasn't working out."

"But, you're okay, though?" I asked.

"What do you mean?"

"Financially ... she didn't ask for money, did she?"

"I'm okay, Timothy," he said. "Don't worry about me."

He said it was his father he was worried about. Mrs. Hiebert had left for the city. This was news to me. I asked how Randall felt about it, but he said he'd already had enough to drink and talking about his parents would cause him to want to drink even more. Then he admitted that his star-anise-golden-syrup IPA wasn't as good as he had been hoping for.

"I'm thinking of throwing it all out and starting over," he said. "Like my mom in the city."

He said his mother was now living in the Exchange District with a retired classical studies professor. Randall said they bought one of those condos on Bannatyne that used to be a warehouse.

"Anyway, I'm still thinking of going to Russia," he said. "I've got to get out of here."

"Svetlana didn't put you off of the idea?" I asked.

Randall paused. "You know very well, Timothy, that this was never really about Svetlana."

I spent the next few days holding a ladder and resisting the urge to send Fart-Joke Thiessen flying headfirst into the snowbank out on Santa Monica Boulevard, formerly Schellenberg Lane. We were told to put out the Christmas decorations right after the first snowfall. "That's when the shopping begins," BLT said at our last town meeting, where we were told to close our eyes and imagine our very own megamart bustling with holiday shoppers right here on our very own Main Street. I assume my vision was considerably less idyllic than BLT had intended.

My job was to stand there and keep my hands on the ladder while the Thiessen kid climbed to the top with a string of Christmas lights dangling behind him like a tail. He also had a few electrified nativity figures tucked under his arms that we were supposed to hang up there somewhere, and I greatly admired his ability to ascend a ladder while holding so much stuff, which radically altered my understanding of the value of having a good, solid Thiessen boy on staff. I could have gone up myself if I wanted—I had seniority—but I was kind of afraid of heights, especially if I had to rely on a Thiessen to hold my ladder. No, staying on the ground and doing the holding was fine with me, even though I did get a couple glass shepherds and a few broken wise men in my face. After a while, the Thiessen boy would come back down and we'd tromp through the snow and move the ladder over a few feet. It took us all morning to just get that one string of lights up.

We also put a Santa and baby Jesus on every vacant lot in town. Mr. Vogt didn't like the fact that the Santas were bigger than the Jesuses, but these were the only Santas

and Jesuses available within our budget. On one of the
lots, we erected a sign that said THE REASON FOR THE
SEASON, but after Jesus went missing a few days later,
we weren't sure that the intended message was being con-
veyed and Mr. Vogt demanded that we move the remaining Santa to one of the other lots. As a result, there was a
place with two Santas and one Jesus, like a bizarre nativity
scene, and another property in town where it appeared
that the "reason for the season" was an empty lot.

When the day came for the Edenfeld Bake Sale and Flea
Market, Katie and I gathered up our Tupperware containers and walked over to the community centre on Crenshaw
near Randall's. The sign said PRETTY PLAIN, of course,
but the *E* and *D* of the former name could clearly be seen
behind the plastic tarp that had been thrown over it. Katie
had put on snowshoes, but I claimed I didn't need them. I
was wrong and after the caked-on snow melted, the bottom of my pants was soaking wet the whole afternoon.
Katie had marched on ahead, however, staying high above
the snow, like she was walking on water, which technically
she was.

When we arrived, I saw that City Sheila had already
radically transformed the appearance of at least three
reluctant Edenfelders, and a few tables were already set
up with pumpkin pie—said to have the highest profit
margin of anything at the sale. There was also an old
man selling antique Clorox bottles and a middle-aged
woman hawking handmade bags from Thailand to
fund a missions trip where she'd walk around Bangkok
praying for both tourists and locals alike. She had paid
for a previous prayer trip to Hawaii the same way. I

observed that there had been no effort made this year to keep the flea market items separate from the baked goods, and was concerned that some folks might lose their appetites having to waddle past rusty tractor parts and mothballed Fortrel pants to reach our table.

At five dollars for a dozen cookies, Mr. Wiebe estimated we'd need to sell twelve hundred cookies to reach our goal of getting a plaque in front of the Elsie Dyck house. Mrs. Friesen had made a sign with her six-year-old grand-daughter that read: *Elsie Dyck Bake Sale. 12pm to 3pm. All are Welcome.* The whole thing was done in thick red crayon, which I suspect was part of Mrs. Friesen's strategy of winning people over with cuteness. Sadly, it didn't seem to work.

"Elsie Dyck made these?" one woman wondered.

"No, no, we're raising money for her," said Brenda from Loans.

"For Elsie Dyck? The writer? Seems like she probably has enough money, what with her book sales and all that."

"It's for her house, actually. Her former house. We want to have a sign put out front. A historic marker, you know?"

"Oh, I don't like that idea at all. Too much foot traffic on Melrose Avenue as it is."

In my estimation, only ten or twelve people pass by Melrose in a day. The last time I drove by, the snow outside the house looked completely undisturbed.

"Well, at least you might want some delicious cookies?" Katie said, holding them up for her to sample.

"Five dollars a dozen? I can make them for cheaper than that."

"It's a fundraiser."

"*Jauma!* That's nearly fifty cents a cookie. Even Frugal Frank's Groceries doesn't charge that much."

"Perhaps you'd like some *tweeback*."

We didn't make that sale.

After an hour or so, we hadn't sold much, and Mrs. Friesen reflected that perhaps next time hand-knitted socks might do the trick. Katie said she was even less confident in her knitting abilities than in her baking.

"My self-worth is not defined by my ability to clothe and feed the next generation. I don't think I—"

"Oh, don't be silly. It's very easy," said Mrs. Friesen. "You can come over one afternoon and I'll show you how it's done."

The crowd thinned out around *faspa* and we were ready to leave, having abandoned all hope of selling our baked goods. Katie and I planned to subsist on nothing but heavily frosted confections for the next couple weeks. However, right before our time was up, and just before the janitor was to come around and rearrange the tables for the evening's Bingo event, Randall walked in the door.

"Got anything left?" he asked.

Brenda from Loans immediately pointed him towards the bowls of *plümemoos* that she had just covered with plastic wrap.

"Do you like this stuff?" she asked.

"I think so," he said. "At least, I'm willing to give it a try."

# Twelve

I suppose some people might find it charming to see their best friend and a heavily tattooed Mennonite woman passed out in each other's arms on an old chesterfield in a garage next to homebrewing equipment, but personally, I found it unsettling. Bare arms. Randall's shirt on the floor. Ulrich Zwingli for all to see.

Randall sure had come a long way since his days of no hand-holding. Much of what I saw before me would have been in direct violation of Randall's very noble standards regarding premarital purity. But then again, maybe not. That's the thing with standards; you can always find loopholes.

I know this makes me a horrible human being, but before rousing the two lovebirds from their slumber, I texted Katie to tell her the news. It's not that I'm a gossip, but

I needed her advice. Should I simply leave them as they lie? Should I wake them and, if so, how should I go about it? Should I leave a note? Maybe wedge it between some glistening limbs and walk away? I had to ask. I guess that's what all the gossips say. "I'm just looking for your advice on what to do about Mr. Goossen and that Schultz woman from across the street. They seem awfully friendly. I don't know what to do. Please help." This is also the strategy they use at church when sharing "prayer requests."

"I found Randall and Brenda," I informed Katie, "in the garage together."

A couple minutes later, no doubt after writing a few more pages of her thesis, Katie replied. "Brenda? You mean from Loans?"

"Yeah, of course Brenda from Loans. What other Brenda is there?"

"What do you mean by 'together'?" she asked.

"In each other's arms. Together together."

She didn't seem to believe me, or still was confused, or wanted to make sure that my "together" was the same as her "together," so I took a photo and sent it to her, so that there would be absolutely no doubt as to what I meant by "together."

"Don't show anyone," I said.

No doubt Katie would be discreet, but there was reason to be concerned for the new couple. When I found them, they'd left the garage door wide open, presumably to cool things down and who knows what kind of gossip had already spread or what photographs had already been taken and then distributed at local quilting bees. Snow was blowing in and a collection of fallen leaves had piled up against the back wall. I was surprised to see that the wind and snow and leaves and sound of passing cars had not disturbed them and wondered just how much of Randall's homebrew they had consumed.

I stood there and stared for a while, noticing that Randall's mouth was open slightly and he was drooling. My intended purpose was to return the cookbook, but even if I'd just left it there, he would have known when he awoke that I'd been there and seen them in that state.

"Just leave them be," Katie said.

Was it even my place to close the garage door?

Surely, I thought, Randall wouldn't want his garage floor covered in dead leaves. That might interfere with his brewing equipment. Besides, it was freezing outside. Then again, maybe dead leaves would improve the flavour of his dreadful IPA. Katie told me to stop being so foolish and just close the door already.

As soon as I pressed the button to close the garage door, the lovers woke up, slowly, I might add, and a little drowsily, but without any shame or attempts to cover their extremities. It was like I wasn't supposed to be shocked at all; it was like I should have seen this coming. They didn't say that, of course, but looked at me and asked how long I'd been standing there.

"Not too long," I said. "What have you been up to?"

Brenda from Loans looked at Randall, then looked back at me.

I told them it was no problem and that I'd delete the pictures.

"You took photos of us?"

Randall demanded to see my phone, which I fished out

of my pocket and dropped on the floor. When I picked it up, the screen looked more cracked than usual, but it was hard to tell.

"Why'd you take these?" Randall said, struggling to decipher through the cracked screen just how incriminating these photos actually were.

"To show Katie," I said. "She didn't believe me."

"Believe you about what?"

Then Brenda from Loans wrapped herself in a blanket and told Randall to calm down and that he had nothing to be ashamed of. She wanted to see the pictures too, and told Randall not to delete them. She said maybe I could even send them to her. I did, right that instant, but I still wasn't sure Randall approved of all this. He certainly didn't seem happy about my prolonged presence.

"I'm sorry. I'll let you two ..." I held the *Mennonite Treasury Cookbook* out for them to see. "Just came to drop this off. Sorry for interrupting."

I placed the cookbook on a bag of barley and backed away cautiously, like I'd been out mushroom picking and had somehow found myself between a mother bear and her cubs. This is an exit strategy I'd learned when in conversation with the Thiessen boys.

That night as I spooned with my fourth cousin once removed, I thought about Randall and Brenda from Loans. I felt a level of satisfaction, like my plans to encourage their romance had inadvertently paid off, all without me having to actually do or say much at all. Perhaps my Edenfeld book could work like that. Just will it into the world without an author.

Regardless, both Randall and Brenda's families would

be very happy when the news got out, not about the hand-holding before marriage, but at the thought that, perhaps, they might spawn some hearty grandchildren. And even better, Brenda from Loans, now evidently in some form of love or lust with Randall, may not ask about our mortgage for months. I slept well that night.

In the morning, I was on salt truck duty. That's what I'd been doing every other day, it seemed. We had to cover the icy streets with sand and salt so that old men in pickup trucks didn't slam into the back of Mrs. Neufeld's Buick. I made sure to slow down at the intersections so that the Thiessen boy I've been assigned to, standing in the back of the truck with a shovel in hand, could toss a bit of sand onto the street and occasionally, albeit accidentally, onto unsuspecting shoppers exiting the thrift store. The sand is for traction; the salt is to melt the ice. Our mixture always included a touch of gravel from the Klassen pits, not because it was necessary, but because Mr. Klassen was on both the town council and the Faith Barn elder board and so was owed an order or two of gravel.

We also had to clear away the snow from the boulevards and the edges of all the properties in town because, in some cases, so much of it had accumulated that when Mrs. Neufeld backed out of her driveway, she couldn't see the oncoming traffic and was doubly likely to get rear-ended. We even had to do the sidewalks, but only in front of churches and the liquor store. "That way everyone's happy," said BLT. All this work meant we weren't tearing down a lot of buildings or trees. It was too cold for that kind of thing, anyway.

It would have been prime ghostwriting season, except

that I'd lost my very last client right in the middle of the project. I was writing one of those Bibles with the little notes on the bottom of every page that tell you what you're supposed to think about what you just read. Reverend Braun interprets every verse as if it's about the Apocalypse. He believes the end is imminent and the Lord could return at any moment, which is why we're supposed to give generously and live pure lives. Imagine the Lord returned while you were getting hammered on Crown Royal and trying to convince the most attractive choir member to climb up into the hayloft with you—how would you explain all that? Initially he had told me he wanted to have the book done "before the Lord returns," but when I asked him when he thought that might be, he said, "It is not for us to know the day or the hour." I told him I'd have the book done before December.

But I never even got to the end of November. Instead, I got an inelegant slap from behind that was somewhere between a pat on the back and a massage. "I'll handle it from here," he told me. He said I shouldn't be too concerned because everything had all been foretold millennia ago, although when I asked for scriptural support he said I would just have to deal with the lack of proof as a sign of the times.

When the start of December rolled by and it became clear to the credit union that our mortgage payments would continue to be sporadic at best, Brenda from Loans called to say there wasn't much she could do to keep them from repossessing our house. I asked her what we could do and she said that what she meant was there wasn't much that could be done by anyone, really. Not even Randall's hand-holding could help us now. We had to break it to my parents that we wouldn't be going to British Columbia for Christmas. We excused our absence by saying we wanted a white Christmas and Yarrow Christmases are much more grey than white. Dad was upset, but Mom said perhaps they'd spend the holidays in Puerto Vallarta with my oil-rich brother.

I dropped off a resume at Koop Convenience and another one at Ernie's. They were open in the evenings and I figured I could pick up a few shifts now that I wasn't doing any ghostwriting. Ernie called me a day later saying that I was overqualified for the job. I think the real reason was because I wasn't a close relative with a tongue stud he was trying to win over to the church with kindness. Mrs. Koop, on the other hand, didn't even reply and the next time I went in there she scurried off to the back room and had one of her employees meet me at the till.

Since my resumes got me nowhere, we spent all our evenings inside, Katie working on her thesis and me expanding the Edenfeld book to an unmanageable size. I'd made a few return visits to the archives and each time I did, Old Stuff Timothy had all this great material for me to include. I just kept writing, adding everything I got at the archives to all the material I'd been given by Mr. Wiebe and Mrs. Ens and Mrs. Friesen. I included all the stuff about the Hiebert barn and the floor patterns and even adapted a few stories from *The Altfeld Book*. There was one about how local women used to tie a bucket to the wagon of courting men they had rejected and the men would ride through town kicking up dust and everyone who saw this spectacle would laugh and know that they'd been turned down. This Edenfeld book of mine had more characters than *War and Peace* and it was only growing. I figured at this rate, if I kept on going, kept on writing, I just might be able to outlast the reign of BLT Wiens. Surely he wouldn't be mayor forever.

Katie was also making progress. She said her academic advisor really liked the work she was doing. "The religio-ethnic culture of Edenfeld is phallogocentric, and derived from the macroculture, but herein manifests a dynamic whereby Anabaptist women are uniquely opaque in both epistemological and linguistic manifestations." That was just the opening sentence.

I rolled my chair beside her.

"I've got seven hundred pages," I said. "Do you really think anyone will want to read this?"

"I'm sure of it," she said.

Then she took my laptop and opened the file, where she scrolled to the top, just below the title and paused for a second before typing.

"A book by Timothy Heppner," she said. "See? It's simple."

I stared at the screen for a while. "A book by Timothy Heppner," I repeated. Then Katie erased my name and said I should do it myself.

"Take some ownership," she said.

I would have done it—maybe—but then Katie overestimated my level of self-esteem and confidence or whatever and decided to reveal the collection of items she'd been stockpiling in the closet. It was a fatal mistake.

"See? There's nothing to be afraid of," she said, then hauled out a garbage bag full of stale loaves that she'd been receiving while I was at work. "We get a new one every day. Well, most days, anyway. Not on the weekends. Not Sundays. There are nasty little notes too. You should see them."

She laughed it all off like it was no big deal, and said she hadn't wanted to show me before, but now was confident that it wouldn't bother me. She had significantly more confidence in me than I had in myself.

She asked me if I wouldn't mind taking the collection to the curb. It was garbage day tomorrow.

I grasped the bag in my hands and stared at Katie.

"You're a brave man," she said, "but we're in this together."

Then she kissed me on the forehead.

It left a mark that I didn't notice until I was brushing my teeth before bed. It was there the whole evening, even when I went out to grab a can of Klik for my lunch the next day. The clerk didn't say a thing. I thought that was rather polite of him, though I'm sure the lipstick generated some rumours. If they were saying that Katie really loves me and that I wasn't ashamed to show it, I'd be okay with that. That's the nicest kind of rumour. I hoped whatever was going around about Randall and Brenda from Loans was equally pleasant.

# Thirteen

One morning sometime after Christmas, during the darkest, coldest, most depressing time of the year, Mr. Vogt called me up to say that my presence was urgently required on Main Street. I looked at my alarm clock. It was seven o'clock and still pitch dark. He explained that one of the Thiessen boys was sick or had gotten his thumb pinched in a beaver trap or something and that I was desperately needed to help "haul away some junk." I'd never considered junk removal to be a particularly urgent task, let alone something that had to occur early in the morning in the dead of winter. Normally, that was the sort of thing we did when the weather was nicer and the snow didn't cake on the tires and the truck didn't need to have its windshield scraped for half an hour before use. I mean, it's junk, so surely it can wait, can't it? That's what I argued, anyway. I also pointed out to him that it was a Saturday, a detail which he readily admitted, but claimed was irrelevant given the urgency of the matter. When I asked him to consider the possibility of doing the job on Monday like a normal person, he said, "That sounds like an Altfeld attitude." I said I wasn't able to work on such short notice.

"I'm kind of busy," I said.

I didn't say what I was busy doing, however, because I was concerned he would argue that the garbage hauling needs of the town of Pretty Plain were more important than sleeping in until noon and then writing an unauthorized history of Edenfeld.

Recently, we'd started eating fried bologna and scrambled eggs mixed with flour for breakfast every morning. For supper too. Katie had also been buying no-name ketchup. I thought if we were so desperate as to buy the off-brand variety, she might as well not bother with the ketchup at all, but she countered by saying the only difference was the packaging and it was all a scam from Big Tomato to get us to overpay. I disagreed. I could spot the generic stuff a mile away. We were rapidly becoming our parents.

Mr. Vogt called again a few minutes later.

"It would be a great opportunity to show your loyalty to the community," he said. "Plus, Timothy, you can earn some time and a half."

My attempts at acquiring an evening job had not been fruitful. Katie, though, managed to get a few shifts pumping gas, a job that we were both very doubtful she would be able to maintain for long. For some reason, the management team doesn't like it when their employees hand out free subversive pamphlets with every fill. "Need your windows washed? Check the oil? Ever read Gloria Steinem?" I agreed to meet Mr. Vogt and whatever remained of the Thiessen boys on Main Street.

I should have known what was up as soon as he told me the address. It was all over. The Hiebert housebarn, the last one in town, was being demolished. I found out later that the town had quietly purchased it sometime that winter after Randall's mother left for the city. With the money from the sale and the destruction of the housebarn, Randall's father was going to spend the winters in Phoenix and the summers out in Yarrow, like my parents.

Why had Randall kept quiet about this? Surely he must have known about it. Maybe he'd even seconded the motion or advised his father on a suitable asking price. He hadn't said a word to me about it, though. We basically only ever spoke about secondary fermentation or "the whole new world" that Brenda from Loans had introduced him to. The last time we spoke, he said he was considering getting a Michael Sattler tattoo on his right bicep.

By the time I got to the demolition site, three sturdy Thiessens, at the direction of Mr. Vogt, had already levelled the barn portion and were making good progress on the house. They were all wearing orange vests over their parkas and were carrying on like it was just any other work day and not one of profound historic significance.

"What's happening here?" I asked.

"What does it look like?" said Mr. Vogt. "Progress."

"Guess we'll finally be getting that megamart after all," said one of the Thiessen boys.

Mr. Vogt handed me the keys to the truck.

"The land's worth quite a bit now," he said. "Gotta cash in while you can."

The truck was nearly full and almost ready for me to haul it away. They made special arrangements with the dump to open up for them on a Saturday. Dump workers don't mind a bit of overtime pay, either.

I hopped into the truck and my Thiessen boy jumped in beside me.

"I'd like to be alone," I said.

In the truck, waiting for the rest of the load, I turned on the radio and listened as a young woman read names in a sombre voice. "Mrs. Gladys Nickel, ninety-two, passed away peacefully in her sleep on Thursday. She is survived by more than two hundred residents of Pretty Plain and was predeceased by her husband Jake who died in a tragic shuffleboard accident in the summer of 2008. In lieu of flowers, donations can be made to the local thrift store ..." I shut it off.

I sat there in silence, my hands gripped to the steering wheel. Despite the cold, sweat rolled down my face. My breath fogged up the windshield and as soon as I rubbed it clear, it fogged right back up again. I could hear the sound of the backhoe, that beeping noise it makes when going in reverse, then a loud crack and a crash, some yelling or perhaps cheering, and then the beeping sound once again.

I didn't really want to look. I didn't want this to be my last living memory of the Hiebert place, but I had to go out and investigate. I opened the door and was greeted with a pile of broken concrete and electrical cords that had been pushed right against the side of the truck. I stepped over it, then surveyed the scene. Broken boards were littered across the dirty snow. In the middle, surrounded by debris, stood the woodstove, still somewhat intact, but now being aggressively handled by two Thiessens with sledgehammers. There was shattered glass everywhere. They hadn't even bothered to salvage the windows. I moved in closer until I noticed something familiar, a splash of colour immediately recognizable as the Hiebert's hand-painted floorboards. I pried a few pieces from the wreckage.

"Get back in the truck."

Mr. Vogt yanked the relics from my hands.

"Those might be worth saving," I said.

He tossed them back onto the pile.

"It's going to the dump with the rest of it," he said.

I managed to save one small piece, though. I like to think that Mr. Vogt saw me take it, but sighed and looked away and, in a tiny but meaningful act of kindness, allowed me this one transgression. It was a fragment, far from intact, of a red flower with green leaves that I slipped into my pocket as I got back into the truck.

By the time the load was ready to be hauled away, the yard looked nothing like it had a day earlier. In fact, it looked nothing like it had for almost a hundred and thirty years. I put the truck in first gear and made my way slowly down the dirt road to the dump. I wasn't stalling for extra pay. I simply couldn't go any faster. When the attendant lifted the gate, I stared at him, empty. He didn't say anything either. We both knew what was happening.

When I returned, Randall was there. I recognized his Audi from a distance, and I thought of stopping or going back, but there were already a few other trucks behind me honking, eager to get the next load, and the road was far too narrow to turn around a truck of that size. I was actually surprised that Randall hadn't shown up earlier, but then again, he's always been the type to slip in at the last minute just before the funeral begins. Or maybe they hadn't really told him about it, not the specifics, anyway. Tearing down the family housebarn is not something you make the relatives aware of ahead of time. It's like putting down the family pet. Better to just go into the bush and get it done.

Randall flagged me down as I pulled up to the lot.

"What's going on here?"

I didn't reply, but looked over at Brenda from Loans in his Audi, who was rubbing her hands together to keep warm.

"What are you doing, Timothy? This place has been in the family since ..."

Again, I glanced over at Brenda. It wasn't that I had anything to say to her, it was just that I didn't know what to say to Randall. Brenda got out of the vehicle and joined him. She put her arm around his waist and the two of them stood there shivering.

"I don't know what to say," I said. "Well, you must have known about it."

"How?"

"You seconded the motion, right?"

Randall dug his shoe into the dirty snow beneath him.

"I'm not sure," he said. "I wasn't paying attention."

Randall and Brenda stuck around for a while, watching me work, but left just before BLT arrived with all the town councillors. They stood at the scene wearing matching parkas with fur-trimmed hoods that they'd purchased with town funds. Each coat had their name on one shoulder and *Town of Pretty Plain* on the other. They lowered their hoods, linked arms, and smiled for their photographer. The photo was in the paper the next week. The headline said: "Make Way for the Big-Box Store!" And that was that.

At the next meeting of the Edenfeld Preservation Society, I knew my presence was becoming increasingly undesirable, and not just because I had forgotten the tray of vegetables and ranch dip I had signed up to bring. We realized this error as soon as we pulled into the parking lot and Katie said I should stay while she ran over to the store to purchase a few half-priced cucumbers and a bag of baby carrots.

"I don't want to go in alone," I said.

Katie escorted me to the basement, peered into the room, then whipped back up the stairs and out the door. When I entered, no one was sitting in their regular spots. Instead, they were all standing, talking in whispers. Even those stopped when they saw me. There was a hush.

"What are you doing here?" said Mr. Wiebe.

"It's Tuesday, isn't it?"

More silence.

"I don't think we're comfortable with this," said Mrs. Ens. "Your kind aren't welcome here."

"My kind?"

"Parks and Wreck! You know very well what I mean."

"It was gone before I got there," I said. "There was nothing I could do."

I looked over at Brenda from Loans, standing in the corner.

"It's not all his fault," she said finally.

Mrs. Friesen approached me. I thought perhaps she was going to slug me. Instead, she reached up and wrapped her arms around me.

"That's it, then," said Mrs. Friesen, her voice quavering as she spoke. "It's all over. Edenfeld no longer exists."

Mrs. Ens tried to comfort her, offering her something to eat, but Mrs. Friesen said she wasn't in the mood for pistachio salad. In fact, no one was. For the first time in Preservation Society history, the food just sat there and I wished Katie wasn't out buying more with our non-existent veggie budget.

"I'm sorry," I said.

There wasn't much reaction.

"I want to redeem myself," I explained, "if you'll allow me to."

I told them that if they would permit me to continue, I would like to finish the Edenfeld book. I pulled out the scrap of flooring I had saved from the Hiebert housebarn.

I passed it around and each person held it silently, until it arrived in City Sheila's hands. She held onto it for a while and then asked if the group members would do her the honour of referring to her simply as "Sheila" from then on. She said she didn't think of herself as a city person anymore. We all agreed and I asked her for the spelling of her last name.

"So I can get it right," I said. "For the Acknowledgements section in the book."

When you don't remember someone's name, Randall says, just ask them how they spell it.

"D-A-V-I-S," Sheila said, spelling it slowly with a pause between each letter. I was embarrassed I'd asked.

"Well, if you'll allow me to continue, I promise to get the book done as soon as I can," I said. "This is something I need to do."

Brenda from Loans said she felt the same way right before she got her first tattoo.

"It was painful and I worried what my mother would think. I was also worried it wouldn't turn out well because I didn't have the money to go to one of those guys in the city and so I got Mrs. Froese's daughter Bethany to do it and she was only starting out. I think I was her second client. There was a lot I was worried about, but I knew if I didn't do it, I'd never do anything."

I nodded and said it was exactly like that. I was willing to put my full effort towards finishing the Edenfeld book, I said.

Mr. Wiebe took this to mean that I hadn't been putting in that same full effort thus far. He lambasted me, calling me a lazy *fül*, before Mrs. Friesen interrupted his rant and said it was time for him to listen for once. She said the church had given her another chance when she wore slacks to the Sunday school picnic in 1981 and if the church could forgive that, then they could forgive me.

Mr. Wiebe, on the other hand, claimed he'd had significant reservations about having a Parks and Rec member in the Preservation Society from the very beginning, and that my behaviour at BLT's speech and this latest demolition had proved his suspicions to be correct. He demanded to see evidence of my work thus far on the Edenfeld book.

I had anticipated this question and went out to my truck to fetch the printed manuscript. It was eight hundred pages long. It took me two trips.

"I don't know what to cut," I said. "So many stories. So many lives. I don't want to leave anything out."

Mr. Wiebe said my sentiment was admirable, but they were paying me to both write and edit and that would have to mean at least a few cuts. He said the Kehlers might be expendable.

Being so eager to toss the Kehlers did not sit well with the others and when they finally put it up for a vote, they decided to allow me to continue with the book. Even Mr. Wiebe calmed down once he was plied with the freshly sliced vegetables Katie eventually showed up with. They said it could be two volumes if need be.

At the end of the meeting, Mrs. Friesen forwarded a motion to remove the word "Preservation" from the society's name, since there wasn't anything of historic value left in Edenfeld to preserve. She said the goal of the society was "no longer simply to preserve, but to provoke."

Katie thought it was an excellent idea and raised her hand as if we were already voting on the motion, which we weren't. Katie said regardless of any vote, she was going to refer to our group as the Edenfeld Provocation Society from that moment forward. But then Mrs. Ens said that changing the name would be the sort of thing that BLT Wiens might do and we should keep the name for the sake of tradition if nothing else.

"Besides," said Sheila, "there's still one building left in town that's worth preserving."

This was something every one of us agreed on.

After a viewing of *The Siemenses of Silberfeld: A Voyage of Discovery,* we held hands and agreed that we would all do our part to preserve the Elsie Dyck house. Then Mrs.

Ens requested that we sing a few verses of "This World Is Not My Home," which had always been her favourite hymn ever since she was a girl.

I was standing next to Mr. Wiebe, who squeezed my hand tightly while we sang, and I couldn't tell if this was a friendly sign of community or a warning that I'd better not go astray again. Then, still gripping my hand firmly in his, he prayed, asking God to give us the grace to accept the fact that our heritage buildings were all but gone and the courage to fight for the Elsie Dyck house. It was an obvious riff on the Serenity Prayer they use in Alcoholics Anonymous, but I didn't point this out as it would only taint Mr. Wiebe's otherwise stellar reputation. I thought he was all done, but then he squeezed me even tighter and asked the Lord to bless my Edenfeld book "and the hands that prepared it" which is usually what people say when they're just about to consume some deli meat.

I thanked him for the blessing, in part so that he'd let go of my hand, but also because, despite the plagiarism, I thought he was sincere.

For weeks after the demolition, Randall didn't leave his garage much and every time I went over there, he was sprawled on the couch, shirt on the ground, Brenda from Loans in his trembling arms. It seemed like I was always interrupting them, even when he had expressly invited me over and they were fully clothed. I never stayed long and Katie didn't show up at all, saying that every second she spent in that depressing garage was a second she could be pumping gas or writing her thesis. Randall and Brenda from Loans seemed to live on that couch next to the malted grains.

I still visited them though, on occasion. I'm not sure why. I just couldn't break a habit I'd had for more than a decade. Besides, Randall was my friend and I wasn't about to abandon him just because he always had his shirt off.

One day I went over and was surprised to see Randall and Brenda from Loans had left the garage and were standing in the snow in front of the house. Randall didn't even give me a chance to get out of my truck. He knocked on the window and I rolled it down.

"We'll just be gone a month or two," he said.

"What? Gone where?"

"We figured we'd do the Trans-Siberian Railway," he said.

"But in reverse," Brenda from Loans said. "I've heard it's better if you start in Vladivostok."

"It's winter now, so it'll be just like it was when half our relatives were sent to the Gulag," Randall explained. "We'll be able to do some research for Brenda's novel. She's got this great idea about a romance between a Soviet soldier and a Bueckert woman."

Brenda from Loans said she had to quit her job to take this trip, but wasn't too worried as they'd probably take her back when she returned.

"I'm tired of fighting," she said, but I didn't ask whether she meant fighting to preserve our heritage buildings or standing up to the credit union's top brass for Katie and me. Maybe she meant something else entirely. She didn't clarify how exactly this Trans-Siberian trip would affect the Elsie Dyck house or our mortgage, and I didn't get a chance to ask because Randall was already handing me the keys and giving me a list of things to do around the house while they were away.

He said I should turn random lights off and on and drive up and down the snow on the driveway a few times each day so it looked like someone was home. He also said I could drink all his beer if I wanted. I thanked him, this time sincerely.

"Well, God bless, I guess," I said.

"Oh, right, God bless."

# Fourteen

On foot-washing Sunday, there was a note in my church mailbox. Usually it's filled with parenting leaflets about the appropriate age to teach your children about tithing, or lists of more wholesome alternatives to secular rock bands. It was in the church mailbox, for example, where I learned that the musical stylings of Henry Heidebrecht and His Hayloft Boys are every bit as good as Nirvana and without the long hair and drums. I have to admit, Mr. Heidebrecht played a pretty mean autoharp. Now, however, there was something else in my mailbox.

It said: *We need to talk. Mrs. Friesen.*

I waited until Katie had finished pumicing Mrs. Epp's bunions and then showed her the note. Actually, I stood nearby watching and she gave me a look like I should back off a bit, like now was not the time to be passing her notes, not with her fingers threaded between Mrs. Epp's arthritic toes.

"The men aren't nearly so thorough," I observed.

"Well, the men get to Heaven in other ways," she said. "For us, it's childbearing or foot-washing, and I'm not about to have a child anytime soon."

All the other denominations just share a cup of red wine and a handful of crackers every now and then, but Mennonites insist that scrubbing each other's feet in a plastic bowl filled with tepid water and sock lint is the only way to paradise. It's our most precious sacrament.

The church entrance was full of puddles from all the melting snow brought in on people's shoes, which they stamped off unceremoniously on rubber mats near the door. There were splashes and stains on the pant legs of the whole congregation and I figured the foot-washing was, at this point, redundant.

When Katie was finished with Mrs. Epp, we stood in the lobby, surrounded by dozens of long black coats and dirty rubber shoe covers, and read the note together. It was a pretty bold move to put a note in a mailbox like that, especially since everything that goes in there is supposed to be approved by the church evangelism committee and is meant exclusively for "the edification of the brethren."

"So, which Mrs. Friesen is this?" Katie asked. "Our Mrs. Friesen?"

It was never a good idea to assume the identity of a Friesen. "Our Mrs. Friesen" was, of course, Mrs. Friesen from the Preservation Society, but there were plenty of other options. I've come into contact with dozens of Mrs.

Friesens in Edenfeld and at least nine of them were in the lobby at that very moment.

I glanced around. Mrs. Leonard L. Friesen? She was conversing with the pastor's wife about the Sunday school curriculum, so that didn't seem too likely. Mrs. H. F. Friesen? She was busy pinching the cheeks of all the children as they filed out of children's church. I tried to make eye contact, but she just kept on pinching. Then there was Mrs. Harry Friesen, a woman whose own first name was a mystery to absolutely everyone, including her own husband, who also referred to her as Mrs. Harry Friesen. She still had her socks off and her feet were wet. I figured it was unlikely, then, that she would have ventured all the way to the mailboxes in that state of undress, and even if she had, it was equally unlikely that she would have been able to complete such a task without leaving a trail of footprints on the carpet. I ruled her out too.

"You can stick around and talk to all the Mrs. Friesens you want, but I've gotta go," Katie said. "I've got to write five more pages on Judith Butler for tomorrow."

Just as we were about to leave, I noticed Our Mrs. Friesen over by the coat rack, struggling to put on her parka among the piles of men's rubber overshoes. She smiled when I looked in her direction.

"You wanted to talk?" I guessed.

"Oh, yes. You seemed busy with Mr. Klassen's corns, so I left a note," she said. "I didn't want to interrupt."

I told her she was always free to interrupt Mr. Klassen's corns. She said she would keep that in mind and then said she had something very important to tell me.

"About the Edenfeld book," she said.

I looked around. This wasn't the place for such conversations. I happened to know that some of the men putting on their overshoes nearby had very high-powered hearing aids.

"Not here. At Frugal Frank's," I said. "In the sausage aisle."

Randall once told me that the best place for clandestine conversations was the sausage aisle at Frugal Frank's. The store was owned by a Lutheran family now, and unlike Ernie's across the street, it was a property that BLT had yet to wiretap. Randall claimed there was something about a good German sausage that scrambled the airwaves for even the most modern surveillance technology. "I think it's the natural casings," he said.

We agreed to meet on Monday evening. I thought it was best if we rendezvoused around seven, during the hockey game when the place would be empty. Mrs. Friesen agreed, saying it wouldn't take long. We might even be able to finish the conversation by the time we reached the *schintjefleesch*.

"So, very quick then?" I asked.

"Yes, very quick then," she said.

When I arrived at Frugal Frank's that Monday, my cheeks were flushed and my nose was red and running. I had walked to save what little gas money we had for Katie to get to university three times a week. I didn't recognize any of the staff except for one woman from church who was stocking the shelves with canned beets. On Sundays, she hands out bulletins and leads old women by the arm to their seats. She knows precisely the row where each person wishes to sit. She is quite gifted.

"You work here now?" I asked.

"Yup. For two years already."

We chatted for a while and I could see from a distance that Mrs. Friesen had already positioned herself near the sausages. I tried numerous times to say "*na jo*" and extricate myself from the conversation, but she seemed bored and talkative and it wasn't that easy to do. Thankfully it didn't take long before someone spilled a bottle of dealcoholized wine in aisle five and she had to go clean it up.

Mrs. Friesen was alone by the liverwurst when I finally approached her. She turned to shake my hand, saying something about how dreadfully cold it was out there. I didn't think we should be seen together, so I looked straight ahead at the tubular meat and pretended I was examining the ingredients for any undesirable additives. Mrs. Friesen stood nearby and acted like she was collecting supplies for next Sunday's potluck. Finally she said, "Be patient, Timothy, like a boiling frog."

"What?"

An elderly couple approached us from behind with a shopping cart full of bran flakes and prune juice. The woman said something in Plautdietsch and pointed to the top row. I didn't understand. The man with her said, "She wants the canned ham. Three containers." I obliged the couple and eventually they made their way to the end of the aisle and out of earshot.

"If I had walked into church in the seventies with a knee-length skirt and a face full of makeup," Mrs. Friesen continued, "I would have been tossed out immediately. But now? Everyone dresses like that. The revolution is slow. It's like cooking a frog. If you toss it into a boiling pot, it will jump out immediately, but if you gradually turn up the temperature, it will slowly be boiled alive."

I had heard that analogy about the frog and hot water before. Mr. Wiebe, who had spent three years studying the evolution of amphibians in his undergrad degree, claimed it wasn't actually true, but Mrs. Friesen said that factual accuracy in this case didn't really matter.

"A metaphor need not stand up to scientific testing," she said.

She turned around to face me. She said she was tired of looking at the liverwurst, and that this was all becoming a bit too much like a spy novel. She said we could probably grab a coffee somewhere. I was about to refuse, to explain about all those stale loaves and nasty notes on my doorstep, when she said, "I know why you've lost so many clients."

Now I turned around.

"Let's just say you've been the subject of considerable discussion at the town council," she said. "They've even got your client list. For the better part of a year, they've been working their way through it, contacting each and every one of them, encouraging them to 'search their own hearts' regarding your services as a ghostwriter."

Mrs. Friesen had obtained this information despite the fact that she wasn't actually allowed to observe the council meetings because she was a woman. Sure, there was a provincial law that meant they couldn't keep her out, but anytime she showed up they'd mysteriously end the meeting early.

"It always became an 'in camera' meeting," she said, "but I have my methods."

I wasn't sure what those methods were, but I assumed

they had something to do with miniature recording devices hidden in potted plants.

"Mr. Harder? And Mr. Loewen? And Mrs. Janzen? And Reverend Braun? And—"

"Yes, yes. I don't need the list," she said. "BLT got to them all. Surely you must have suspected as much. I think at first they were only hoping to discourage you from churning out all those family histories, but when they found out that the Society had hired you to write an Edenfeld book, well, they upped their game."

"Katie and I have been eating nothing but fried bologna for months!"

Mrs. Friesen told me to keep my voice down.

It wasn't that Mr. Harder and Mr. Loewen and all the rest didn't like my writing, and it wasn't that they had found someone cheaper; it was pressure from BLT, plain and simple. He had rid the town of novelists and house-barns, and now, it seemed, he was going after ghostwriters. Well, ghostwriters who didn't second him in town meetings, anyway.

"There's no way I can finish the Edenfeld book now," I said. I saw my face, defeated, reflecting back at me from the glass in front of some prime cuts of steak. I told Mrs. Friesen about the menacing loaves I'd been receiving.

"Oh, I know about those," said Mrs. Friesen. "Elsie got those for months before she left town. You got the notes too?"

I told her I did.

"Listen, Timothy. They're doing this because they think the book will have a real impact," she said. "You have to complete it … and you have to publish it."

My knees were shaking. "That's it," I said. "I'm finished."

A teenage boy came by with a bucket and mop that he slid back and forth in front of us before saying "excuse me" and swerving around us.

"Can I help you find anything?" he asked.

Mrs. Friesen asked him where the Jell-O was and he said it was probably in aisle seven next to the dried fruit and marshmallows. She thanked him and commended him on his excellent mopping.

On our way to aisle seven she said, "Why don't you go speak with Elsie Dyck?"

I stopped.

"Elsie Dyck? What do you mean? She's …"

"Oh, she's around," Mrs. Friesen said. "The food court in the city, remember?"

She handed me a jug of pickling vinegar and told me to take it to the till.

"It wouldn't look right to walk out of here without buying anything," she said. She gave me a fifty-dollar bill and told me to keep the change.

"Thanks," I said. "For the vinegar … and the money. Things are really tight and I—"

"Don't give up. Speak with her," she said. "Go on a Sunday afternoon."

I didn't know whether to believe her, or where she might have obtained this information about Elsie Dyck, or whether it had anything to do, yet again, with her surveillance abilities. I walked home with the vinegar under one arm and a gloved hand alternating between each ear. It was freezing.

When I arrived, Katie was working at her laptop. She

hadn't gone to the hockey game either. I placed the jug on the coffee table and said we'd probably be able to preserve some of those green beans Mrs. Ens had given us. Katie said they weren't fresh from the garden at this point anyway.

I sat down and told her what Mrs. Friesen had said about my clients and about BLT and how he was, of course, the one responsible for all those threatening loaves at our front door. I rested my head in my hands, then opened my computer. Eight hundred pages. It had been a lot of work. Months of writing.

"I could just delete it all."

Katie rested her head on my shoulder. "I know you wouldn't do that," she said.

I sighed. Katie and I stood up and looked at each other. She reached up and ran her fingers through my hair, then dragged me to our bed, which was still unmade from the morning. When my jeans came off, a few quarters fell to the ground and I remembered, at that very inopportune moment, the money that Mrs. Friesen had given me, which I had crumpled up and wedged into one of my front pockets. Forty-five dollars and some change.

"That's enough to go to the city at least twice," I said.

I told Katie about Elsie Dyck and the food court and she said I should get dressed again and go to the mall right then. I said the mall would probably be closed by the time I got there.

"I promise I'll go, though," I said. "Sunday."

For the time being, I was glad the mall was closed. Katie kicked my jeans aside, pushed me to the ground, and kissed me like only a distant cousin can.

# Farjoah

# Fifteen

Katie's been standing up a lot lately. In church, I mean. There's a ten-minute time slot in the Sunday morning service when anyone can grab the mic and request prayer for various things. The farmers have been asking people to pray for a "slow melt" this spring. You can also ask the congregation to get on their knees for your troubled niece who has started listening to rock music or dating a Catholic. Katie's stood up four weeks in a row now, which is unusual for her. Not that she doesn't believe in prayer, but I guess she's probably gun-shy about sharing after the time I mentioned to the congregation how grateful we were that Katie "just got her bachelor's" and the rumour spread that she was leaving me for a younger man. There are still some people who look at me and whisper like I'm the town's most notorious cuckold.

"We don't want to lose our house," she told them.

Reverend Broesky interrupted her and said she should say her name, even though everyone at South Edenfeld already knew her, but it was all under the pretense that the prayer would be more effective if people could ask by name.

"Katie," she said. "Timothy's wife."

Then she explained that we'd been going through a difficult time. I think she called it a "dry spell" so the farmers could relate. She explained that the ghostwriting business had been slow and that BLT's salary cuts to the town's employees last year certainly hadn't helped, and that the credit union had already begun the foreclosure process. "But somehow," she said, "if we could get a bit of money, maybe we'd be able to keep the house."

I kept my head down, too embarrassed to meet anyone's eyes.

"So, if you all could pray for us about that, it would be very much appreciated," she said. You're always supposed to ask for prayer when really what you need is a bit of cash.

Then Katie took her seat and handed the microphone to the usher who tapped on the top of it to test it for the next person and there was a loud screech from the speakers that freaked out the sound guy.

We had been contacted by somebody named Allan, Brenda from Loans's replacement at the credit union. He said we'd have to come up with money pronto or they'd take the house. "People are eager for that spot," he said. "It would make a great location for a dollar store."

Katie was still on shaky ground at the gas station. She wasn't subtle about her pamphlet distribution. She didn't slip them in with a backroads map or a fishing license or something; she handed them out openly and directly and her manager told her that if she did it again, she would be let go. They said this was completely unacceptable behaviour and that her job was to fill tanks and make sure the Bergmans weren't stealing anything and that's it. "We don't allow proselytizing here," her manager said, or rather yelled, so as to be heard over the gospel music that was blasting from the gas station's speakers. Apparently shoplifters are deterred by "The Old Rugged Cross."

After the service, Dorothy the librarian pulled me aside and said she'd be praying for us. She had recently started attending South Edenfeld when they said she could have free reign over the church library. She gave me a cheque and told me to wait until I got home to look at it because it wouldn't be appropriate to examine such things in a church lobby. I wanted to take it to the credit union right away, to buy us some more time, but played it cool, knowing full well the place was not open until Monday at ten. Then a few others came by with fives and tens and offered to bring our troubles to the "throne of the Almighty." A child—I don't even know his name—handed Katie three quarters and a nickel. She would've turned it down, but she didn't want to deprive him of the opportunity to give. She found Mr. Wiebe, who was counting the offering in the church office, and added the eighty cents to the pile. He asked her if she wanted a tax-deductible receipt.

I skipped the potluck that Sunday. I felt bad about taking the money and running, but it was Sunday and Elsie Dyck was waiting, or might be anyway, and I had to save my appetite for whatever they were selling these days at the Snow View Mall food court. I made a brief stop at home. Katie said if I was going to venture out in weather like this I'd better bundle up and bring along my phone in case of an emergency. "You don't want to be stranded out on the highway," she said, tossing me a wool toque her grandmother had knitted. I put it on, examined myself in the mirror briefly, and told her not to worry. I said there were plenty of snowmobilers zipping along the ditch on Sunday afternoons and if need be I could always flag down one who didn't look particularly intoxicated.

At first the roads were actually pretty clear and I figured I'd be chowing down on a plate of pad thai with Elsie Dyck in no time. The snowplows had just been through and except for a few moments stuck behind a Dodge Caravan turning left into Ste. Adèle, I was able to make good time. Unfortunately, it didn't take long before I caught up with the aforementioned plows, which were backing up traffic for almost a full kilometre. I hadn't counted on this. There's an old joke we tell around here about the Altfeld man who swims halfway across a lake before turning back once he realizes he probably won't make it all the way. However, heading back home doesn't seem like such a bad idea when the blowing snow in your sightline and big yellow truck in your path are preventing you from approaching anywhere close to normal highway speeds. After half an hour of this, I gave up and turned back towards Edenfeld. When I got home, I looked at my gas gauge. I was all right. I would be able to seek out Elsie Dyck another day.

Back at home from my ill-fated trip to the city, Katie and I decided to spend the rest of the afternoon at the Dick Plett Library using the Wi-Fi. BLT had recently ordered all

Pretty Plain establishments to open on Sundays. He said it
was a prerequisite for getting a megamart.

Agnes was sitting at the front desk knitting. The library
wasn't busy and Agnes complained about having to work
on a Sunday, saying it was the Lord's day and that only
servers in restaurants should have to slog through it on the
Sabbath. We were disappointed that Dorothy wasn't there
because we wanted to thank her for the cheque (and for
praying), but according to Agnes, Dorothy hadn't worked
a Sunday shift in weeks. "Not since she got put in charge
of that church library," she said bitterly. Her mood lifted,
however, when she saw the opportunity to teach Katie how
to use the personal computers to search for synonyms of
the word "subjugation."

When I checked my email there were three spam mes-
sages about male virility and a forwarded article about
western alienation from my brother in Alberta. There
was also a lengthy note from Randall. I deleted the others
without reading them, but opened Randall's. He said he
might be in love with Brenda and that Siberia was much
nicer than all those forced childhood screenings of *Doctor
Zhivago* had led him to believe.

He told me that since they'd arrived, he and Brenda
Formerly from Loans had been having quite the time.
They'd stopped for a while in the city of Omsk where they
both got jobs teaching English. Hopefully they'd earn
enough money to get to Moscow and fly home. This all
seemed very irresponsible to me, but then, Randall always
says I don't take enough risks. "Your parents are living it up
in Yarrow like a bunch of college kids," he says, "and you
and Katie are sitting there in Edenfeld like an old retired

couple." I don't take criticism very seriously coming from a man whose idea of a holiday is a few weeks in a sketchy apartment somewhere north of Kazakhstan.

Randall had no teaching experience or any qualifications, but he said the English school had overlooked such deficiencies since he agreed to work very long hours for very little pay and take a spot in one of the less-desirable locations like the outskirts of Omsk. He told them he'd lived in a less-than-desirable location his entire life.

He'd managed to find some renters for his place in Edenfeld—some construction workers from the city who agreed to keep their cigarette smoking to the back-yard—and having Brenda Formerly from Loans with him really helped since they could split an apartment and thus double their net income to, like, sixty thousand rubles a month or something. I have no idea what that translates to in Canadian dollars, but judging from the pictures of the apartment they're holed up in, it's probably not as substantial a figure as it sounds.

I replied to Randall's email with a photo of Agnes from the library helping Katie use the space bar. The look on Katie's face was priceless. I asked Randall to pray and consider sending us a bit of money if they had any extra rubles.

The next Sunday, the roads were much better and I still had half a tank of gas remaining and a bit of cash left from Mrs. Friesen. I figured I'd have just enough for an order of kung pao chicken, especially if I didn't get the egg rolls and stuck with tap water. In Edenfeld, we call this "city food." After decades of home-cooked meals where every ingredient is fresh from the garden or a mason jar, food courts are something of a treat for us and I'm sure BLT is working on a plan to make sure the town of Pretty Plain has plenty of them.

The Snow View Mall food court was busy. I tried to find a good place to sit so I could scope things out and perhaps spot someone, anyone, who looked like they might be a long-lost Edenfeld literary icon. There weren't many seating options except for one table that I shared for a few minutes with a woman who was changing her baby's diaper. Someone had left a half-eaten plate of chili fries and I was tempted, by my ingrained notions of thrift and my desire to deviate from my diet of fried bologna, to take a bite, but decided there were too many people around who might be witnesses. Instead, I just tossed it all into a nearby trash bin and wiped the remaining crumbs off the table with a napkin. Then I got in line to order my kung pao chicken.

"I'll have a number six, please," I said, "and a side of rice."

At first, there was something wrong with the debit machine so when I tried to pay it kept rejecting my attempts. Embarrassed, I got out a credit card, and then a second one, and finally, after none of these methods worked, I used up the cash from Mrs. Friesen.

By that time, the table I'd cleared was occupied, so I looked around for someplace else to sit. I thought of asking an elderly couple whether I could join them at their table for four, but decided against it after I saw them leaning in for a kiss. I didn't want to intrude. I stood around holding my tray until someone gripped me by the wrist.

"Did you discard this woman's chili fries?"

It was a security guard. He looked about seventeen years old.

"Oh, I didn't realize …"

I tried to explain the situation and how it really wasn't a situation at all, and that I'd be happy to purchase the offended party another order of chili fries. The aggressive young *benjel* left me for a moment and began chatting with an older guard, presumably his supervisor, who then told me that I unfortunately needed to leave the premises.

A few people put down their pizza slices and turned in our direction. I didn't want to be manhandled or escorted from the building, so I told them I was leaving "and never coming back." I would have made good on my promise too, if it wasn't for the fact that at that very moment Mrs. Friesen miraculously appeared. Skeptics would probably say she had been in the crowd of dishevelled mall-goers the whole time and had simply been using the facilities, but true believers, like myself, have no choice but to attribute her appearance to an act of the divine. She emerged from the heavens and told the security guards there was no need to detain me. "Everything is all right, officer." They left without causing any further trouble.

"They really like it when you talk to them as if they're the police," she said.

She laughed and told me I should join her at a table at the other end of the food court next to the taco place where it was quieter. We wound our way through the crowd and made it to the table relatively unscathed, other than the brief moment when my head narrowly missed a Greek salad.

I sat down across from Mrs. Friesen, slunk my shoulders, and took a deep breath. Someone sat down next to me.

"Hello," I said, turning slowly in their direction.

"Don't worry," the stranger said. "I got myself some more chili fries."

"Timothy, meet Elsie," said Mrs. Friesen.

"Elsie? Elsie Dyck?"

Of course it was, but please forgive me for being a little shocked. Yes, it was Elsie Dyck that I'd come to see, it was Elsie Dyck who I had been expecting, but this was one of those situations where I didn't expect to have my expectations met. Considering they ranked among the best chili fries in this particular food court, it was also unexpected how gracious she was about my disposal of them.

"Excuse me," I said, pulling out a book from the fancy cloth book bag Katie had given me and staring at the dust jacket photo. I wasn't even subtle about it. I looked Elsie up and down, then back at the dust jacket, my mouth agape the entire time. She had changed, but not much, really. Certainly not as much as thirty years might suggest. She had pepper-coloured hair and glasses hanging from her neck over a bright blouse that they would never have allowed in Edenfeld back in the nineties.

I shook her hand as if to test that she wasn't a mirage. This was the very same hand that wrote *Scandalous Quotations from a Mennonite Diary*; the very same hand that wrote *Pilgrim at Edenfeld Creek* and *A Doll's Housebarn* and all the rest. I told her I'd never wash it again and she laughed and laughed as if no one had ever made such a clever comment to her before, although they most certainly had.

"It's an honour to meet you," I said. "I can't believe it's you."

"You want to check the spear wound in my side?" she asked.

I said that wouldn't be necessary.

"We were wondering when you were going to show up," said Mrs. Friesen. She said they'd been on the lookout for me. She said she'd been meeting Elsie at the mall every Sunday for years.

I slammed back half a cup of tap water. Then out came a nervous barrage of questions. Was she working on anything new? Where did she get the inspiration for the enigmatic plumber in *Scandalous Quotations*? I loved that character, I said. What really happened with BLT? And what about her bakery? Were her sugar cookies really tainted? Why did she spend so much time in the food court? I rattled off these questions, rather aggressively—too aggressively—and eventually Mrs. Friesen had to apologize to her friend for my behaviour.

Elsie leaned in to sample a piece of my kung pao chicken. It was quite the honour.

"Why do you think I come here?" she asked.

I didn't want to say what I really thought: that she was down-and-out, that she had no other place to go, that maybe going to some tasteless suburban mall every week was the one glimmer of excitement she had in a life that had been all but obliterated by the actions of Edenfeld's fanatical mayor.

"I really can't imagine," I said.

"I come here," Elsie said, "for the same reason you go to Ernie's."

I was shocked that she knew about that. Mrs. Friesen smiled at me.

"To observe," Elsie continued. "It's as simple as that. If you want to know what city life is like, just look around you. This is a great place for any writer. There are potential characters everywhere."

She leaned in, the glasses around her neck dangling dangerously close to my kung pao.

"I hear they've been putting stale bread on your doorstep," she said.

I swallowed hard and said that they had.

"Same old tactics," said Elsie, shaking her head. "Well, you know if they do that, Timothy, it means you really do have to publish your book now."

I looked at her and took a breath, hoping she was kidding.

"But they ruined your life," I said. I repeated what I'd heard about BLT and the health inspector and the mass poisoning and how she was never allowed to set foot in town again. I said I really didn't want that to happen to me.

Elsie laughed.

"Those are just the stories he tells. That man is not nearly as powerful as he claims to be," said Elsie.

"He's just the little man behind the curtain," said Mrs. Friesen. "He's the Wizard of Oz."

I'd never thought of him like that before. It was probably the sort of thing that occurred to Katie and maybe Randall, on occasion, but when your very livelihood is being stripped from you, the man behind it all hardly seems benign.

"He's more like the Wicked Witch of the East," I said.

Elsie Dyck reminded me that the Wicked Witch was crushed by a house.

"Believe me, Timothy, I left town completely of my own volition," said Elsie. "By 1994, I was done with Edenfeld. Yes, I was sad to leave; there are still a lot of things I like about that town. For one thing, it's full of storytellers. There are people—some of them, anyway—who truly care about what Edenfeld means today and has meant over the years. You don't see that as much in the city here. But after *Scandalous Quotations* came out, I was done with Edenfeld. I needed to find other stories in other places. I had moved on. BLT had nothing to do with it."

I breathed more calmly now and could feel my anxiety subsiding.

I looked down at my copy of *Scandalous Quotations*. Actually, I'd brought along all five of her books, in the off chance that she really would be here and maybe she'd be willing to sign them. I kept the other four hidden in my bag, however, not wanting to impose too much. I placed *Scandalous Quotations* on the table and she said, "Of course I will," before I even asked. I dug through my stuff looking for a ballpoint pen, but Elsie pulled one out of her pocket and said a writer always has one with her.

Then she flipped open the cover, paused for a moment to think, and wrote, *Pay no attention to that man behind the curtain,* and signed her name.

"I can sign the other ones too, if you'd like," she said, pointing to my bag full of her novels.

By then my kung pao chicken was cold and I went up to the vendor and asked for a takeout box so I could reheat it later. I didn't want it to go to waste. It was time to grab my food-court poultry and go.

I'd like to say that Elsie Dyck ascended into the troposphere or something, but instead I waved and watched from my seat as she and Mrs. Friesen weaved their way through the crowds, past the place that sells bath bombs and vanilla-scented body cleansers, and then disappeared out of sight.

As soon as I stood up, a young couple approached and stood nearby carrying shopping bags they were eager to deposit. I packed up my stuff, glancing at Elsie's signature once more before I closed the book carefully.

"Pay no attention to that man," I whispered. I told myself that I wouldn't forget those words. I'd look at them every day, maybe rip the page out of the book and pin it on the headboard next to the genealogy.

When I arrived back home it was dark outside. Katie turned on the outdoor light as I pulled into the driveway. The sidewalk was icy and the door was frozen shut. It was always frozen shut. I stood there banging on it for a while before Katie came to help out.

"You have to kick it at the bottom," she hollered through the frozen door. "That's where the ice builds up."

This was a common occurrence in the spring when everything would melt and then temperatures would dip again at night, and every time the door froze shut Katie would tell me the solution was to give it a kick. On one occasion, we were stuck inside the house and Katie was worried she was going to be late for work. There was some talk about breaking a window to escape, but we sat down and calculated that the cost of a broken window would far exceed whatever financial loss there may be from a missed shift at the gas station, so the idea was quickly scuttled. When I emailed Randall about this recurring problem, he replied that I needed to replace something called "weather stripping," but I hadn't a clue what that was and I figured kicking the door was much more efficient and cost-effective. "Was there weather stripping on your old house-barn?" I asked. He told me not to mention it. It was gone now and he didn't like to think about it.

Katie kept yelling at me through the closed door. "Kick it, Timothy. You have to kick the door to loosen the ice." So I kicked and pushed and she pulled on the doorknob from the inside and then, a moment later, there was just this hole where the doorknob had once been and Katie peaked through the circle and said she thought it might be broken. The door was still frozen shut.

This time, we had to smash a window, I said. It was freezing and I wasn't going to wait for Katie to melt the ice with the blow dryer.

"You can't break a window, Timothy," Katie said. "We have to be able to sell this place, remember? Well, the credit union does, anyway."

I stood there shivering while Katie cranked the heat on the blow dryer and eventually I was able to push the door open. She looked at the paper takeout box in my hand; the sauce had leaked and was now frozen to my fingers.

"Kung pao chicken," I said. "Do you want some?"

Katie said she did and popped it in the microwave.

"Did you meet Elsie Dyck?" she asked.

"I threw out her fries," I said.

Katie turned around.

"She was there?"

I showed her my signed copy of *Scandalous Quotations* and explained about the inscription. Then I stacked up the other books that she had signed for Katie, who excitedly looked at each and every signature and then said, "You know, these are probably worth something, and we sure could use the extra money."

I looked at her, shocked, before she smiled wide and placed each book carefully on her shelf next to the complete works of Virginia Woolf.

"So, what are you going to do now?" Katie asked.

I booted up the file on my computer and in size twenty font typed: THE UNAUTHORIZED HISTORY OF EDENFELD, MANITOBA. Then I added: A BOOK BY TIMOTHY HEPPNER.

Katie slung her arms around my neck.

"It's not quite finished," I said. "I have one more chapter to write."

# Sixteen

Once the snow began to melt, people were worried there might be flooding, and not the fun kind like when Noah gathered up the cute little animals and left all the humans, save for his own righteous family, to perish. No, I mean the nasty kind of flooding, like when the river overflows into all the canola fields and you have to drive far out of your way just to get to Eigengrund so you can get your hands on some delicious Hutterite chickens. The forecast looked pretty bad.

For all BLT's negative talk about Altfeld, the one advantage it has over Edenfeld is that it's a little farther from the river. The flood waters never reach it. Not that Edenfeld is exactly on the river, either. Our early church elders didn't want us to be too close to any transportation methods that might give us easy access to the city. There is a well-known story about an Edenfeld elder who entered the river on a raft and then floated north to the place where the Red River met the Rat. He was supposed to meet delegates from the old country who were thinking of bringing their people over. Instead, he was whisked away, never to be seen again, and the delegates brought their people to Kansas instead. I included this story in my book, which is bound to be problematic for BLT who will no doubt find offense in the notion that anyone might consider Edenfeld a second choice to Kansas. It's true, though—Edenfeld is always at risk of flooding in the spring and with the snow we'd received this year, it wasn't just the farmers who were concerned it might melt too quickly.

So it was a bit of a shock when, despite the imminent threat of flooding, BLT called me in to talk about my book.

"Just a pleasant chat with me and the rest of the town council."

I had just finished the last chapter. It was a departure from the others, which I'd titled "The Unauthorized Future of Edenfeld, Manitoba." Not the past. Not a history. The future. It was forty pages of dystopian speculation, describing Pretty Plain in the year 2120, when it's just another suburb of the city, where people live here at night and take the train to the city every day, where everyone speaks English, where there's a megamart every few blocks, where there's not a single woman in a long homemade dress or a single man in a black hat and suspenders, where we all just buy whatever they sell us at the mall, where we eat chili fries every meal of every day, where every house is the same boring bungalow and all the grass is perfectly manicured, and all the streets are paved, and all the trees, and any sense of history and identity, have vanished; like we're all living in some terrible, giant suburban mall food court.

Katie loved the chapter, but I was fairly certain BLT would not feel the same way.

The meeting was supposed to be held at the town hall, but it was under construction to give BLT a bigger office and a front desk where you could walk in and pay your water bill or complain about the neighbour with the unleashed dog. I thought that maybe the meeting could be delayed until the renovations were complete and the flood waters had subsided, but BLT said things had "gone on long enough yet" and he had found a room in a dark, damp corner of the Faith Barn basement that was more than adequate for our purposes.

Katie and I didn't often walk in the direction of the Faith Barn. When we did, though, we always stopped at the old cemetery and speculated about the lives of people who were only known as a name on a headstone, many of which had been toppled by vandals and were covered in lichen. There are a few Heppners buried there, but none are close relatives. *Gerhard Heppner, 1847-1918. Aganetha Heppner, 1881-1903.* Perhaps fourth cousins once removed, at best.

"Are you ready for BLT?" Katie asked, crouching down to examine one of the headstones. Another Heppner.

I said I wasn't sure.

Katie said that wasn't good enough, that I needed to be "ready for battle," and I said I figured I was about as prepared for battle as a pacifist ever could be. I certainly didn't want to end up like all those other Heppners in the Edenfeld Pioneer cemetery, not yet anyway.

When we got to the Faith Barn, Katie entered with me and said she'd wait in the lobby for my impending martyrdom. I sneezed. There was sawdust everywhere, left over from their annual Faith Barn Gospel Hoedown. Katie blew me a kiss as I clenched my fists and walked downstairs. In the basement was a large open area, presumably used for floor hockey and potlucks. Along the wall were all the Sunday school rooms, but every door was closed and the whole thing felt a bit like "The Lady, or the Tiger." Then I noticed a thin sheet of paper on one of the doors that said *Pretty Plain Office*. BLT had taped over a more permanent sign that said CHURCH DISCIPLINE. Evidently this was also the same room that doubled as the nursery on Sunday mornings. I knocked, opened the door, and peered in. I was instantly met with a whiff of baby powder.

I was five minutes early, but the meeting had already started. There was a prayer and then the a capella singing of a hymn, which was not ideal considering there were only seven of us in the room and five were tenors. We did all four verses of "A Mighty Fortress Is Our God," which was an ominous sign. Nothing good ever happens after you do all four verses. It always sets such a serious tone. They invited me to sit down on one of those cheap, wooden church-basement chairs, whose entire *raison d'être* comes from the fact that they're good for stacking.

"Ah, you're here, Timothy. Have a seat."

There they were, the councillors, all wearing black suits, sitting in a row like a hand of Rook cards. The beards were gone. BLT had sent out a memo that town officials were to go clean-shaven from now on. I scratched my face, not having shaved in a couple days myself, and took a seat in the chair they had set out for me. I folded my hands on my lap like the elders do when they sit in front of the congregation on Sunday mornings, judging the parishioners.

We sat watching each other for a while, taking mental notes, and then BLT shifted in his chair and cleared his throat.

"I understand this book of yours is a Preservation Society initiative, correct?" he asked.

I hesitated. "Well, yes, but, well, as you can see ..."

I stood up and heaved over my manuscript to him. It was thick. Nine hundred and thirty-eight pages. I hadn't been able to reach a thousand.

He looked at the first page.

"Yes, it's got your name on it."

BLT flipped through the pages briefly.

"Only one copy?" he asked. "We'll have Anne run off a few more."

He held up his arm as if hailing a taxi and, just like that, the secretary appeared. I hadn't noticed she was in the room. She gathered up the manuscript and left.

We waited for quite some time. At one point, Anne returned and informed us that unfortunately she had run out of paper and needed to go over to the Lutheran church across the street to see if she could procure some more. BLT told her to "make haste" and she did just that. The elders and councillors stared at me without saying anything. I figured we could have at least talked about the price of flaxseed or something. Nothing. Eventually, though, they started speaking softly to each other in Plautdietsch.

"English, please, gentlemen," BLT said.

When Anne finally reappeared, she wheeled in a cart

stacked high with copies of the book and she distributed one to each of the town councillors. They looked at each other, then at BLT, then filed out of the room like ducklings.

"We'll let you know within an hour."

I thought an hour was awfully quick. There was no way they were doing anything more than skimming, unless they were speed-readers, which, I can say from hearing them read scripture and committee reports, was definitely not the case.

BLT said I could help myself to some sugar cubes, which I was supposed to dip into coffee and suck on while I waited. I didn't, figuring that increased glucose levels would only impede my readiness for battle. He closed the door behind him and left me alone. This was hardly the military engagement I had anticipated.

I sat in that wooden chair, nervous, but in some sense relieved. It was finished. There was no going back. No more skulking around. I had nothing left to hide. My name was on the book and that book was in BLT's hands. I wondered what sections they would read. Would they just glance over the table of contents or look for their names in the index? Would they even make it to the last chapter? I was proud of what I had accomplished, but I was also quite anxious. I wondered what the consequences would be for me, for Katie, for our future here in Edenfeld when they discovered what was in those pages. A lot of it would embarrass them. There was also a lot that would not be conducive to business. And that final chapter. Well, I could practically hear the big old paper shredder being fired up in the other room already.

True to their word, the councillors re-entered after an hour. Fifty-eight minutes, to be exact. I stood up and saw Katie standing in the doorway. She walked over to stand beside me and offered me her hand. She didn't even wait for the councillors to take their seats.

"He spent months on this," she said. "You have absolutely no right to treat him this way!"

The men sat down and looked at each other, saying things like "highly irregular" and "unprecedented" and "why, I never." They explained that Katie would have to leave because this whole matter was between me and them, but she refused and stood at my side.

I spoke, more timidly than she did, and said, "I really hope that you'll reconsider."

One of the men said they weren't going to continue with the meeting as long as Katie was still there, but BLT said maybe it was okay this time, since that's the way they do it in the city. "They even had a woman mayor once," he pointed out.

The rest of them murmured amongst themselves for a bit, then nodded in unison. The meeting would continue.

"I really hope you'll reconsider," I repeated.

BLT smiled at me and adjusted his tie. "'The Unauthorized Future of Edenfeld'?" he asked.

"I'm pretty proud of that chapter," I said. "I worked very hard on it."

He muttered something to one of his compatriots.

"It should be 'The Unauthorized Future of Pretty Plain,' should it not?"

"Well, I guess so, but I—"

"That chapter's title needs tweaking. Don't you agree?"

BLT walked over to me, paged through the manuscript, grabbed the first nine hundred pages, and handed them to me and Katie.

"Do with these what you will," he said, "but this last chapter I'm going to keep."

"I have other copies, you know."

"I don't doubt that," he said. "Just tweak the title."

"What?"

"Listen to what we're saying. Just change the title of this last chapter." He stared at me. His breath reeked of star anise. "Just change the title," he repeated. "You'll need to anyway, since it's not unauthorized if we approve of it, now is it?"

Elder Peters piped up. "'Pretty Plain: City of the Future,'" he said. "How does that sound to you? You know, this book could be of promotional value. A real boost. What a glorious vision of the future you have presented us."

"I don't understand."

"Listen, Timothy," said Elder Peters. "We like the book, the part about our future, anyway. We think it could be valuable to the community. It'll give people hope. Something we can all work towards. Like a mission statement."

With that, the elders stood up, and ushered me into the church kitchen where they offered me raisin buns and cheese curds—the same food they serve at funerals. We ate for about an hour, during which time there was much encouragement and aggressive handshaking and I was as confused as I ever have been in my entire life. Katie kept her distance, though I saw that she cringed every time one of the councillors gave me a side hug.

"If things go well with the Pretty Plain book, I think you'll see a real surge in that ghostwriting business of yours," said Elder Peters. "We've discussed it as a council and we'd like to get this book published as soon as possible. Well, the last chapter at least."

"Publish it?"

"Yeah, we'll print up a few copies for you. You can invite the neighbours. We'll even provide the pickles."

Katie approached us, saying it was time to go, and all the men said things like "of course, of course, don't let us keep you," and "we'll be in touch." I'm glad Katie came to my rescue, because by then I had fully exhausted my ability to smile and pretend to take a compliment.

As we were about to leave, BLT cornered me in the hallway.

"Oh, one more thing there, Timothy," he said, gripping my hands in his. "I've been looking for a new seconder. How do you feel about attending a few meetings?"

# Seventeen

Even with the help of the historic atlas he bought at the used book sale, finding Old Edenfeld was not an easy task for Randall. There had been three in Prussia, a couple in Ukraine, and at least one more in Siberia, but none of these were listed on modern maps. The tattoo that covered Brenda's entire back and mapped all the abandoned Mennonite colonies of the Russian Empire wasn't much help either and Randall's attempts to examine it with a magnifying glass were met with extreme opposition, he said. Randall knew from the historic atlas that there had been a village called Edenfeld between the rivers of Irtysh and Om. He said they would try to investigate. "I know it's not our true ancestral home, exactly, but it might be the only Edenfeld left." He had a lot of ground to cover. Omsk Oblast was a large area and getting to the potential village involved hiring a guy with gaping holes in both his English vocabulary and the floor of his rusty Lada to go down some roads that didn't exist except in this man's vivid imagination. Randall said it was a long journey, and uncomfortable, but he was pretty sure they found the place after three days with Anatoly and the expenditure of a sizeable sum of cash. Randall had not been able to procure the services of a real historian or archaeologist or anything like that, but he was confident that Anatoly had found some sort of abandoned village site in rough proximity to a place marked "Edenfeld" in the atlas.

Randall kept sending me pictures of the place. Usually Brenda Formerly from Loans was standing in the photos smiling, cigarette in hand, and taking up most of the frame, but I could get a general sense of it. There were a few run-down homes. Randall said the foundations of some buildings were made from headstones raided from an old cemetery. No one was living in the houses anymore and the yards were full of weeds, the roofs caving in. At least they didn't take them down with a backhoe. Historic buildings probably last longer in Russian neglect than in BLT's brand of Canadian progress.

I told him about my consultation with town council, though I held back on some of the details, knowing full well that the Internet chats on these personal computers at the library were closely monitored.

"They want to publish it," I said.

Randall told me it was a "golden opportunity" to showcase my talents and make a few mortgage payments, but I couldn't tell if he was joking. I didn't ask, not wanting my question to be flagged as suspicious, so I let him tell me more about his new life in Siberia.

He said he had learned more than fifty words in Russian. "*Nyet, da*, the whole works."

He had been in touch with the Russian farmer who owned the Old Edenfeld land, or rather, he shook his hand while Anatoly spoke to him. Randall didn't have any clue of what was being said because fifty words only gets you so far and when they're speaking fast it gets you nowhere at all. Randall asked if there was anyone left in the region who spoke Plautdietsch and Anatoly looked at him and said he didn't know how to translate the word "Plautdietsch" into Russian. Randall took it as a pretty clear indication that the answer was no.

They seemed to be having a good time out there, though, teaching English on the weekdays and spending their weekends acclimating themselves to the local vodka and discovering old, abandoned Mennonite villages. He said he was even thinking about distilling some vodka of his own and I didn't dissuade him from the task. They're thinking of staying there for a while, maybe long term, if the guy in charge of the English school bribes the right person to get a visa extension.

"Russia's going places," Randall said. "Up."

We tried to use the video chat but the library computers weren't adequate for the task and after resetting the modem and logging in again with the help of various elderly librarians, I chatted with Randall for a few more minutes before he reminded me of the time difference and said he had to go to bed. Brenda Formerly from Loans was calling, he said.

All of this was of great interest at the next Preservation Society meeting. Everyone was curious to see Randall's photos from the old country and Mrs. Friesen, our resident expert on the colonies of Siberia, said that Randall may actually have located the last remaining Edenfeld.

"Of course, it's impossible to say for certain," she said. "Unless we do some soil analysis."

"*Oba*, Sarah, you think soil analysis will prove everything," said Mrs. Ens. "It's not so simple as soil analysis. I'd much sooner trust diary entries than anything that soil analysis can dig up."

Sheila didn't know much about soil analysis and diaries, but asked whether I might be able to get a few more photos from Randall.

"Some without people in them would be nice," she said. "To give us a better sense of the lay of the land."

Mr. Wiebe agreed. "People help us *nuscht*."

Then he rambled on for a while about the state of Russia today and how, although he had never visited the country himself and had no doubt that it had improved since the Soviet days, he suspected it wasn't nearly as nice as Randall had described.

"He's a pawn in their game, I'm afraid," said Mr. Wiebe. "Oh sure, they'll lead you around on some tour of the old villages. They'll take you to what you want to see, but they don't show you the whole truth. They'll tell you 'oh, yes, this is Edenfeld' and 'this is Hoffnunghorst' and 'yes, indeed, this is the place where the Janzens had their estate or where the Lepps kept their chickens,' but who knows for sure."

Then, in a segue that I'm certain was deliberate, Mr.

Wiebe said, "And speaking of pawns, how about that Edenfeld book you're writing, Timothy? Seems that BLT Wiens has taken over the project."

"That's not a very gracious comment," said Mrs. Friesen, though she didn't deny its validity.

I handed them the first nine hundred pages, everything but the last chapter, which I explained was in BLT's possession at the moment.

"It's about the future. It's fiction," I said. "It doesn't paint a pretty picture."

Mr. Wiebe struggled to cradle the manuscript in his lap.

"I still think it's a little long, but it's certainly an upgrade on *Edenfeld: A Town of a Thousand Horses*," said Mr. Wiebe. "Did you manage to get in the story about old 'Corner' Kasdorf who was excommunicated back in '65 after a pool table was discovered in his basement?"

I hadn't come across that story.

"Well, never mind. Save it for the next edition," said Mr. Wiebe. "This is some good work you've done here."

I collected the pages and with Katie's help, we shuffled them against the table until the edges were nice and flush.

"He let me keep these," I said, "but he wants to publish the rest. The last chapter. You know, my nightmarish vision of Edenfeld's future? I'm not sure if I should let him go through with it, though."

"You must!" said Mrs. Friesen.

I was shocked at her enthusiasm, but she was persistent.

"BLT might not understand what it means," she said, "but others will."

Sheila said she moved out here for a reason and did not relish the idea of Edenfeld becoming just another suburb.

"I could have just stayed in the city if all I wanted out of life was quick and easy access to a megamart," she said. "Let them publish it, Timothy."

After that, Mr. Wiebe wheeled in the television for the evening's movie. We were going to watch a marathon of short films about Mennonite gardening, including *The Pesky Wiebes on My Neighbour's Lawn*, *Flower Power: The Story of Mrs. Buhr's Begonias*, and the definitive classic of Mennonite animation, *Peter Penner Picked a Peck of Pickled Peppers*, when the power went out. Well, the TV went off anyway, and Mr. Wiebe, try as he might, could not figure out how to get it back on again. We ate all the snacks, but there was no movie. The technical difficulties were attributed to the devil trying to interfere in the Lord's business, or perhaps it was sabotage from BLT's posse, and Mrs. Ens pointed out that those could be considered one and the same.

As we were preparing to depart, Katie said, "We're going to need to get some sandbags around the Elsie Dyck house."

Residents of Edenfeld had been asked to start filling sandbags. We'd been told this was only a precautionary measure and that the flood was not going to be as bad as feared and might only affect a few basements here and there. However, to be on the safe side, we were asked to prepare as many sandbags as we could and put them around our yards to keep the water out. But there wouldn't be anyone to put sandbags around the Elsie Dyck house.

"On an open market," said Mrs. Friesen, "the land is probably worth as much as the house. BLT would be happy if the place flooded."

Thankfully, we had some time, but not much. There was still snow on the ground, lots of it, but it was starting to melt and we all knew that once the ice on the river melted and then all the snow melted into the river, things could get nasty. Mrs. Ens said her grandchildren were coming over this weekend and she'd recruit them to fill sandbags. Mr. Wiebe expressed doubts about this plan since Mrs. Ens's oldest grandchild was only seven and, according to Mr. Wiebe, the young lad had never done a proper day's work in his life.

"When the time comes," Mrs. Friesen said, "we'll save Elsie's house."

A few days later, I threw on a pair of rubber boots and splashed my way through the puddles to meet BLT at the place where they print the books around here: Cornie's Print Shop. Cornie himself is long dead, but the name is so iconic in these parts that Edenfelders refer to anyone that works there as one of "*Tjnals siene Tjinja.*" BLT was standing at the counter when I arrived, chatting with a young woman, one of "Cornie's children," whose painful grimace made it all too clear to anyone other than our esteemed mayor that she would have preferred that he sat down on that chair over there and kept quiet, rather than pontificate in great detail about the mill rate. The bell above the door chimed when I entered and they both turned to greet me.

"Timothy, you have some decisions to make."

He took me through a door that was marked STAFF ONLY. The girl looked hesitant, but since he was the mayor and owned the building where Cornie's Print Shop was located, she let him through.

"The most important thing about book publishing," he said, "is selecting your plastic spiral binding. What colour do you want?"

I was shown a long row with every colour in the (admittedly limited) Mennonite rainbow, and selected a black spiral, because I figured it would draw the least attention. I didn't think people should be focusing so much on the binding and should, instead, be trying to get what they could from the text.

"The black one is fine," I said.

BLT scoffed.

"Is 'fine' all you want out of life, Timothy?"

He vetoed my selection. He had that power. It was written in the local constitution or something.

"It's better to have something that catches the eye," he said. He held out a red spiral, waved it in my face, then put it back. "Green might be better," he said. "It doesn't stir up the urges quite as much."

I told him, "Fine, yeah, whatever. A green plastic spiral binding then. Let's go with that."

Then he saw that they also had blue, a couple different shades of it, including one that BLT said looked too close to black and one that looked too much like the tight Wrangler jeans that the women in the Faith Barn worship band wear, so that was quickly nixed too. The man had real trouble making up his mind. Eventually he settled on a bright orange spiral binding, chosen because it matched the chorus books at church.

"Orange it is," he said. "People will love it."

Next, I needed some kind of cover. We went back into

the office where the girl was waiting. She seemed relieved when we returned.

"Let me see the covers," BLT said. There is no graphic designer on staff; Cornie's had employed one about ten years ago, but a headhunter over in Altfeld offered him two dollars more an hour to work restoring floor patterns in all the local housebarns. So, instead of any kind of custom design, Cornie's offers a selection of pre-made covers. It's like choosing an ice cream cake. Most of the choices are schlocky inspirational designs with sunsets and beaches and lime green font. I thought they might clash with the orange spiral binding, so I chose a very plain cover that had a black font and no beaches. Now all that was left was to provide a picture of myself and a short biography for the back cover, which BLT recited to the girl at the desk who wrote it all down on a pad like we were ordering a roast beef dip.

"Timothy B. Heppner is a Mennonite writer from Pretty Plain, Manitoba. He has extensive experience ghostwriting memoirs for aging citizens. He lives with his wife Katie in an unkempt bungalow with no pets and no children. *Pretty Plain: City of the Future* is his first publication."

It was okay, though I thought perhaps the bungalow shouldn't be mentioned since we might not be living there much longer, but BLT said I had nothing to worry about in that regard.

"You're in the Lord's hands now," he said, by which I think he meant his own.

He said I would be able to take a cut from the profits and that it would be more than enough to cover a few mortgage payments.

I took a photo of myself wearing glasses that I got from the thrift store, because I thought authors should wear glasses. I attempted to do a selfie, but then BLT intervened and said it would be much better if he took the photo. It wasn't.

And that was it. We were given a glossy printout that showed exactly what it would all look like when it was published for real. On the cover it said *"Pretty Plain: City of the Future* by Timothy B. Heppner."* It was that easy. The girl behind the counter handed me the bill, or was about to anyway, before BLT seized the paper and ceremoniously stuffed it into his breast pocket.

He seemed sincere; he was really looking forward to getting my "wonderful new mission statement" out into the world. The entire process took less than thirty minutes, not counting the hour we spent discussing plastic spiral bindings. BLT, however, was particularly impressed that he would be able to make it back home in time to catch the tail end of the "Back to the Bible" broadcast.

"Oh, yeah, me too," I said.

# Eighteen

The day of the book launch, Mr. Vogt said I could leave at lunch and let the Thiessens finish pressure-washing a winter's worth of cigarette butts and dog poop off the sidewalk in front of the community centre. He said I should go home and prepare since it was my "big day." I did what he said, reluctantly, but I honestly would rather have been on my hands and knees scrubbing the sidewalks with the Thiessens than agonizing all afternoon about my impending book release.

The whole town knew about it. BLT had sent a letter, penned by his secretary Anne who had been expertly trained to mimic his handwriting, to every household in town encouraging them to "come out and witness the future of Pretty Plain." He even sent my picture along, calling me a "promising new voice in civic planning." I pulled up a chair next to Katie at the kitchen table and rested my chin on her shoulder, but I didn't even look at the copy of. my book she had sitting there open in front of her. I had nothing to plan. I would go there, read a few sections, sign a few copies, and then escape out the back. I didn't want to think about it.

After an afternoon of me asking her about her thesis and kissing her on the top of her head every few minutes, Katie was tired of me pestering her and demanded that I "stop being so antsy" and go on over to Ernie's already. She said she'd go with me. BLT had booked Ernie's so that those who didn't get his letter might pass by in the melting snow outside and maybe glance through the window and see me reading while they went to pick up their cabbages for this week's *komst borscht*. I expected the place to be packed.

We arrived an hour early—too early—but at least it gave Katie plenty of time to carefully stack the spiral-bound books on the table, ready for the signing afterwards. One copy was supposed to be displayed upright so people could see all the effort we put into the cover and the spiral binding and all that, but whenever Katie tried to get it to stand on its own, it would flop over. Eventually she abandoned the idea and made a large pile like a stack of training manuals and the whole thing looked like a set-up for a CPR course.

I stood nearby, nervously rubbing my hands together and thinking about how later that afternoon, for the first time in my life, people, real people, would read my writing and know that I wrote it. They'd see that my vision of Edenfeld's future was not a pretty one. I might as well have been straightening historic signs in the clear light of day. "All I can do," I told Katie on the way over, "is hope at least some of them will understand what I am trying to say."

I had to invite the Preservation Society members myself, since their invitations had been "lost in the mail." In reality, invitations had not actually been sent to everyone in town as promised, but only to those who were on the mayor's list of "registered supporters" who always received an intimidating phone call on election day to "get out and vote."

There was still half an hour to go and Sheila offered to touch up my blemishes. I hadn't realized I had any blemishes and said that if they were there she might as well do something about them. It took quite the effort to get me looking presentable and it didn't help that Katie was sitting nearby the whole time cracking jokes. "Out, damned spot! Out I say!"

Mrs. Ens was there too, surreptitiously pushing her baking on everyone who looked even the least bit interested, while Mr. Wiebe moved the chairs around because the current arrangement was not to his liking. Surprisingly, Ernie was rather hands-off with the seating arrangement this time. He seemed preoccupied with making sure there were enough coffee creamers for the mayor and all the other dignitaries who were expected to attend. He seemed happy to let Mr. Wiebe take charge.

"How many do you want in a row?" Mr. Wiebe asked me. "Do you want an aisle in the middle?"

He held three stacked chairs under each arm as if to show off his strength and youthful vitality. Katie said an aisle in the middle was too much like church.

"There won't be an altar call," she said.

It was best, she explained, if he just made ten rows of eight, which would give the women a place to put their purses and the men the space to spill over their seats without bothering anyone. Mr. Wiebe questioned whether to have such long rows because people might have to slide themselves past each other and Edenfelders have always preferred not to make physical contact with other human beings if at all possible.

As soon as the first row was set up, I let Katie and Mr. Wiebe continue to get things ready and plopped down on a chair next to Mrs. Friesen. She held my hand for a moment to comfort me. I thought it was sweet, but also a little clammy. It wasn't her fault—the clamminess—it was all me. After a while, I pulled my hand away and wiped it on my pant leg. I smiled at her.

"Elsie sends her regards," she said, breathing the words into my ear. "Don't worry. People will get it."

I wasn't so sure about that. The crowd had been hand-selected by the mayor, after all. I said I would be satisfied if I wasn't rounded up and tossed on the pyre with the elms.

Finally, it was about time to start. I turned around and glanced at the crowd that had started to trickle in. BLT was standing in the back laughing with three old men with sunglasses perched on top of their heads. One of them gave me a thumbs up, a gesture I hesitantly reciprocated. There were about thirty people in their seats at that point and a few more milling about drinking coffee and chatting. There was some commotion over the fact they had run out of decaf and one woman said she'd just have some hot water rather than caffeinated coffee, but Ernie said he didn't have any hot water ready and it would take him a few minutes to boil some and the woman said, "Fine, then I'll drink the regular coffee, but if I don't get to sleep tonight, I know who to blame." Ernie said he was all right with that and recommended that she take a jog down by the feed mill to burn off the caffeine.

After a few more people sat down, BLT Wiens went to the front to introduce me. There was no microphone—it wasn't seen as necessary—but there was a podium that he leaned on until it wobbled and he backed off, fearing a repeat, I assume, of his disastrous speech at the opening of the Edenfeld Roller Rink in the spring of '97.

"Thank you for coming," he began. "I first got to know young Timothy Heppner when he was hired to work on our beloved Parks and Recreation crew a few years back. I'll be honest. I didn't think he had what it took. He was skinny and his hands were smooth. He didn't look like the sort who could handle the rigours of demolition work. However, Mr. Heppner surprised me. Pleasantly, I must say. He took to the work with zeal and, after checking the records earlier today, I can confirm that Timothy here has been directly involved in the clearing of more land in our fair town than anyone else in the past ten years. He's a real progressive. Little did I know when I hired him, however, that this young man with an incredible talent for tearing down old junk would also have such a fine gift for wordsmithing and a brilliant mind for civic improvement. You may not know this, although I suspect some of you may have been his clients, but Mr. Heppner here has ghostwritten many of the family histories and genealogies that adorn our bookshelves. On top of that, he has also published numerous articles in some of our local church newsletters. And so it was only natural that we, as a town council, tasked young Timothy to write a promotional book for our community and I spearheaded the effort to get this book into print.

"Some will say that this book is a work of fiction, but what marvelous and inspirational fiction it is! It tells the tale of a handsome young mayor named Mr. Krahn, bearing an uncanny resemblance to the late actor Edward G. Robinson, who heroically confronts an evil underground organization called The Preservists who are trying to undermine progress and send the town back to the Dark Ages. And the result? Pretty Plain of the year 2120 is a fully fledged bedroom community for the stars, a city, as Timothy puts it, 'that boasts more parking space than any other town in the entire country.' Let me tell you, if I have anything to say about it, it's not going to take as long as that. *Pretty Plain: City of the Future* is a story of community, progress, and, above all, hope."

Then BLT snapped his fingers and one of the men with sunglasses came forward with a life-size cardboard cut-out. Of me. I was holding the spiral-bound book in my hand and smiling. My teeth were whiter than they had ever been.

BLT called me to the front. I squeezed in next to the cut-out, which I had to push to the side by a couple inches so I could stand squarely behind the lectern. The three of us—BLT, myself, and my cut-out—stood there silently for a moment, before BLT nudged me to proceed. And so, I looked out into the audience, opened the book, and started to read.

"My job is to make sure the jerrycans are full."

I paused. What should have been a significant moment in my fledgling literary career was interrupted by the sound of coffee mugs crashing to the floor. Ernie's young employee had overestimated his ability to stack and carry a loaded tray of dirty dishware back to the kitchen. They were cleaning up broken glass for a few minutes and by the time the mop came out I decided it was safe to continue. I looked up at the crowd. Mrs. Friesen was grinning from ear to ear. Mr. Wiebe clapped slowly and silently. Sheila touched her face and smiled, seemingly to indicate that my blemish coverage had turned out okay. The elders stood in the back wearing black suits with their arms crossed. I felt a bit like Captain von Trapp distracting everyone while the family escaped out the back. Katie motioned for me to continue.

"I'm sorry, let me start over," I said. "My job is to make sure the jerrycans are full."

Again I stopped and took a deep breath, and I continued like this, starting and stopping, for quite some time, until Katie rose to her feet, moved my cardboard cut-out off to the side, and stood beside me. She offered me a glass of water. It was exactly like the bumbling testimony I read before my baptism. Katie put her arm around me and smiled.

"My job is to make sure the jerrycans are full," I said. "They always have to be full. It sounds like an easy task, but three young men before me were fired for letting the volume of gasoline drop to unacceptable levels and a fourth kid was axed for forgetting the matches. We don't tolerate that kind of incompetence around here. There's a lot on the line when you're setting housebarns ablaze."

I was going to read more, but BLT looked at his watch and initiated an applause. I think he also paid someone to whistle. A reporter from *The Rubbernecker* crouched in front of me as if to take a picture, but before she could, BLT plowed his way into the photo. Echoing Katie, he slung his arm around my waist. Later, when I suggested to the reporter in a text message that the photo could be cropped by one-third, she took it the wrong way and cut out Katie, although if you looked closely, you could still see her well-manicured fingernails digging into my side.

After the reading, I sat at the table and people lined up to get their books signed. Ernie announced that everyone should purchase the book first and then come back for the autograph, but BLT said, "No, these people are trustworthy," then told Katie to stand by the exit and watch to make sure no one snuck out without paying.

"You've got mortgage payments to make, don't you?" he said.

I didn't know what to say to people or what to write on the page. I guess that was one of those things that I should have planned ahead of time. Maybe I could have done some brainstorming while scrubbing the steps at the community centre. But I had nothing prepared, so I wrote on every single one, *Thanks for coming out. Timothy Heppner,* and one time, in a misguided fit of adventure, I wrote, *All my love,* but immediately stroked it out and made a big mess on the page.

I grabbed a fresh copy and told Mrs. Martens I would start over from scratch. *To Mrs. Martens. Thanks for coming out. Timothy Heppner.* She thanked me and said she remembered when I was only a young boy and how I used to recite Bible verses in front of the whole congregation and how I always did such a great job. "I knew you'd make it in the world," she said.

A group of men approached and I asked for each of their names, even though I knew the first one was a Mr. Goertzen and the second one was a Mr. Plett. Nevertheless, I didn't want to mess up and have to toss out another book. "Who should I make it out to?" I asked and wrote, *Thanks for coming out*, and Mr. Plett wondered why on earth I had written that.

"I'm here all day anyway," he said.

"Well, thanks for buying a book," I said.

Then he turned to Mr. Goertzen and whispered that he didn't know he'd have to pay for this thing.

Now it was Mr. Harder's turn. I was happy he'd shown up at the launch. His granddaughter Emily helped him walk over to my table. I told him I was glad to see him, and I meant it. He leaned down on the table and Emily grasped hold of him as if he had fallen. He brushed her away and leaned in even closer.

"I can't believe they let you publish this," he said.

I looked around. BLT was dumping about four or five creamers into his coffee and laughing it up with some of the town council.

"Take another copy," I said. "It's on me."

When the crowd had thinned, Mrs. Friesen approached the table with a book for me to sign. She said she was eager to take it home and read it. I wrote a few words thanking her for her support and encouragement. She smiled and then grabbed a second book from the pile. "For a friend," she said. I didn't know what to write in this one. I thought maybe something about a man behind a curtain, but I figured that was unoriginal by now, and so, after deliberating for a while, I wrote, *There's no place like home,* and signed my name.

Once the chairs were all stacked, Katie and I walked home. I took a few copies with me, including one to mail to my parents in Yarrow. "They're in the Dominican right now," Katie reminded me. "They'll be there until the end of April." I figured I'd mail it to them at the resort. "It's kind of a beach read, don't you think?" I also planned to mail one to my brother on the oilfields. I knew he wouldn't read it, but he could throw it in the glove compartment of his F-150 and show it to people whenever they opened it up to grab the cannabis he stashed there. I also took one to send to Randall and Brenda Formerly from Loans.

"Two copies," I corrected myself. "Just in case things don't work out between them."

As we walked home, I held the books in one hand and Katie's hand in the other. She looked up at the open sky.

"The trees used to make a canopy across this street," Katie said. "At this time of year, the leaves would be just starting to bud."

We had to weave around a few puddles on the sidewalk and eventually ventured well onto the street to avoid them. We turned down Sunset Strip.

"I guess I'm a real writer now," I said. "My name is on the cover."

"You always were," Katie said.

As we passed 553 Melrose, a truck drove by and we had to jump back onto the icy sidewalk, where we narrowly avoided being drenched by the driver who just cruised on through the puddles as if he hadn't seen us. The sidewalks were covered in ice, and I fell flat on my face, sending all my copies directly into one of the many puddles.

We picked them up, dripping, and made our way home. When we arrived, Katie managed to get them back into respectable shape by laying them out on the kitchen island and playing very loud punk music to speed up the process. When they were dry, the letters on the cover had run together to read "*Petty Pain.*" The spiral binding, however, remained completely intact.

# Nineteen

The custodian at South Edenfeld told me we're going to need a new bulb for the overhead projector. After my book launch, Reverend Broesky was so impressed that he gave me my choice of ministry opportunities, and I figured overhead duty was a step up from going downstairs with the children and sticking paper cut-outs of Bible characters on a huge board made of flannel. We'd recently tossed the hymn books; the pastor said we were losing too many people to the Faith Barn and had to do something to stem the tide. Now my job was to write out the song lyrics on the transparencies beforehand and then do my best to keep up with the music and display the right pages at the right time during the service. Katie sits next to me to make sure I don't mess it up. It's quite the responsibility. They don't give the job to just anyone. I'd even had to get a criminal record check and a credit report and thankfully, after making a sizeable payment and receiving a stern warning, Allan at the credit union said I had now reached the "minimum financial standard required to handle the overhead projector." It was a brand new machine and they were worried someone was going to try to pawn it.

According to the church custodian, though, we'd already used the projector so much that the bulb was wearing out.

"It's going dim," the custodian said. "Won't be long now."

I never noticed, but he said that when he stood at the back of the sanctuary and looked up at the words, sometimes he couldn't make heads or tails of them. I told him I thought it wasn't necessarily the bulb that was the problem, but he insisted it was. He said he'd be able to have a new one by the next Sunday.

The man kept hovering nearby, peppering me with questions about the inner workings of the church overhead projector business. He pointed out a few transparencies that were not displaying the proper copyright information and said the estate of Keith Green would be mighty upset if they ever found out. He also asked me about my technique and how I avoided getting ink on my fingers. "I don't," I said. I was trying to go through all the songs and make sure everything was organized, because it confuses people when the chorus is displayed during the verse part. I was trying to do a good job, but this man wouldn't leave me alone, even though I was certain there was probably a spill in the kitchen he could be addressing. Finally, he sat right next to me.

"I read your book," he said.

I put down the transparencies.

"Oh, yeah, well, Pretty Plain's glorious future, right?"

He shook his head and said no, it didn't seem all that glorious to him.

"It's not glorious," he said, "but it's true."

Then he told me he was buying copies for all his friends, plus a few to give away as presents. I thanked him for his interest. It was nice to know someone was getting it, but then, janitors are like that. They're like bartenders. They know what's up.

I went to Frugal Frank's the next day to check the local bestsellers list which always comes out on Mondays. It's prominently displayed right above the frozen Red River pickerel. Number two. Not bad. I was right below *How to Fast and Pray* by Reverend Peter Berg, which has never been dethroned after nearly five years on the list. I sold one hundred and five copies in the first week alone. BLT was very impressed by the brisk sales and wrote me two royalty cheques, which he made me pick up when I seconded for him at the next council meeting.

Thankfully I haven't had to second anything awful. The worst of it was a motion to drain the water from the outdoor pool after a recent contamination and refill it with clean, undefiled water provided by the Giesbrecht family. No one was actually using the pool this early in the year, but the Giesbrechts had to be kept happy. I also seconded a modest salary increase for town employees, which included bumping up my own wage just a touch above the poverty line.

Most fortuitous for our financial outlook, however, was

when BLT released the parking brake on my ghostwriting career. I picked up three new very enthusiastic clients within a week of my book launch. All three projects were works of fiction, including one that involved a "big city punk rocker named Alexis who abandons it all to live with a handsome Mennonite farmer on the Canadian prairies." BLT even took down all the out-of-date ads for the women's knitting circle in order to make a space on the bulletin board for the enormous poster he had printed for me. This one contained no spelling errors. He offered to let me take home the cardboard cut-out, but only once books sales died down, which he promised would not be for many months. We finally got our Internet turned back on and Katie was able to quit her job at the gas station, or I should say, she deposited leaflets about oral contraceptives under the windshield wipers of every car in the parking lot and got herself canned.

The next time I chatted with Randall, I was comfortably at home and in a state of undress that I wouldn't have dared to attempt at the library, at least not with Agnes or Dorothy around.

Randall told me they were planning to stay in Russia, if possible. He said I could come out for the wedding, though I should be prepared for bumpy roads and wildlife. I wasn't sure why he'd felt the need to warn me about things that were also rather common in our part of the world too.

"It'll be a real Russian wedding," he said.

I told him his wedding with Brenda Formerly from Loans would not be a real Russian wedding since neither of them were actually Russian. He reminded me about how our ancestors had lived in the region for a while and, apparently, that gave him license to adopt any Russian traditions as he saw fit.

"We're even going to have those squat dancers," he said, "but I'll warn you, there's plenty of vodka at Russian weddings. It's pretty harsh stuff. You should start now if you can. Work up to it for the wedding."

I told Randall I wasn't the only one who had something to work up to for his wedding day.

Randall said I was being "unnecessarily obnoxious" and concerned about things that were none of my business and that I was beginning to sound exactly like the Barkman sisters at the quilting bee in Edenfeld, always sticking their noses where they didn't belong, but then I wondered how exactly he knew about the goings-on at the quilting bee and I also asked him to delineate for me precisely what level of obnoxiousness he found tolerable. He didn't reply for a long time, and then finally, I got a new message.

"I really hope you come to the wedding," he said. "You could be my best man."

I said I would think about it and told him he better hold off on the wedding until I could save enough for the tuxedo rental and the Aeroflot flight.

He sent me a photo of a wooden sign he had put up on the Old Edenfeld site. I told him it might be better to call it "Last Edenfeld" rather than "Old Edenfeld" because "Old Edenfeld" implies there are others around that still use that name. The sign said in Russian and English:

ABANDONED IN 1937
ON THIS SITE WAS THE VILLAGE OF EDENFELD
ONE OF MANY MENNONITE SETTLEMENTS
IN THE AREA

In the picture, Randall is standing on one side of the sign with his hand resting on top, while Brenda stands on the other side, squinting as if the sun was in her eyes. In her hand was one of the books I'd sent them. I printed off the photo and put it on our refrigerator next to the garbage pick-up schedule and the latest church bulletin.

"What did you think of the book?" I asked.

"I can't believe they let you publish it," Randall said.

I told him that wasn't the first time someone had told me that.

"Did it achieve what you were hoping?" he asked.

I said I didn't know.

"You don't know what you were hoping to achieve or you don't know whether you've achieved it?"

"Both," I said.

Randall said maybe someday in the future people would read it and understand. He said that's the thing with books: they aren't always appreciated immediately. I knew this was true. It was certainly the case with most of the family history books we wrote, which were usually tossed in a box and only taken out again long after the author had passed and it was too late to ask any questions. I told Randall it was too bad about my Pretty Plain book because spiral binding was not known for its longevity.

I asked if he'd made any friends over there in Russia. He gave the impression that he had, but even if he hadn't, he and Brenda were getting along famously and she was all the company he needed.

"And vice versa," Randall continued. "But like I said, I'd love for you and Katie to come out here for the wedding. It's not like you'd expect it to be. Omsk, I mean. The pictures don't do it justice. It's peaceful, you know? The simple life."

I wondered how a city of a million people could possibly exceed Edenfeld in simplicity.

"It's less ..." He paused for a moment. "It's less concerned."

I said if Katie and I could scrounge up enough money we'd show up for the wedding, especially if he and Brenda were expecting a child or something.

"I'd love to be an uncle to your children," I said.

Randall said there was no risk of that, but said it was a nice thought since that meant he and I were brothers.

"We probably are actually related, you know," I said. "I know a guy who has a computer program where you type in any two names and it tells you—"

"I know all about that program," Randall said. "That's how I knew it was safe to marry Brenda."

Then he asked me about the flood forecast and I told him it wasn't looking good and BLT had us filling sandbags whenever we weren't fixing potholes in front of one of his businesses. There was a long pause and then Randall sent me a message filled with typos that said he would love to stay and chat about prairie flooding, but Brenda Formerly from Loans was luring him to bed with one of her tattoos. It was the same thing that Katie did to me with her Joy Division T-shirts.

I didn't chat with Randall again for weeks. We had

water in our basement, only a few inches, and Mr. Vogt gave me permission to use one of the town's pumps during my lunch break to suck it all out of there. It took me all afternoon and I had to forego a few hours of pay to get the floor dry again. Thankfully my laptop and Katie's collection of late-seventies punk albums escaped unscathed, but we did require new carpeting and I calculated that I'd have to write at least one more book of poetry for Mrs. Esau to pay for the damage.

Once the snow melted, the fields around Edenfeld were all under water and if it wasn't for the dike around town, we would definitely have had a problem, or at least a bigger problem than we did have. There were sandbags around most of the homes because nobody actually trusted BLT's dike, and there was water in the streets, too much of it, but not enough to prevent us from driving to the convenience store to stock up on beef jerky and processed cheddar.

Thankfully our truck was high off the ground, but the guy who bought Randall's Audi was having real trouble and I often heard him coming down the street because water had gotten up under the car and made things wet that weren't intended to be wet and so there was squealing and squeaking every time he hit the brakes or made a sharp turn on Rodeo Drive.

The Parks and Rec crew spent a whole day at the town hall planting flowers. Mr. Vogt said the town was "more than prepared for the flood waters" and so we should now focus our efforts on beautification. "It's good for morale," he said. He also said something about the town hall being on higher ground, but I wasn't sure if he meant topographically or spiritually. One of the Thiessen boys had this idea that we could spell out the words "Pretty Plain" in white daisies on the front lawn outside the town hall. "We can use yellow for the vowels." He had seen this in a magazine. We spent about three hours on the project before we realized that at the size we were making it, we only had enough flowers to spell "Pretty" but decided that was too on the nose. The Thiessen boy said we could do it all over, "just a bit smaller." He said that this time he'd do precise calculations, but he hadn't brought along his calculator and no one trusted his mental math abilities, so we gave up on the idea. Besides, if we did it any smaller, the seniors on the third floor of Golden Slumbers wouldn't even be able to read it.

"They're watching us now," I said. "See, look."

Two women put down their knitting and yelled something at us through the window, but I couldn't make out what they were saying. Then a man approached and I'm certain he said, "Workin' hard or hardly workin'?"

I always answer, "Working hard," as if it's a real question, because you never know when someone's going to complain their tax dollars are paying for people like me to slack off. After that, it was decided that we'd have to lay out the flowers in rows like we normally did.

When my shift was over, I stopped at home and microwaved some frozen soup. Cabbage *borscht*. I took a shower, which was probably unnecessary considering my plans for the evening involved sloshing around in the mud, but it was a force of habit. I was supposed to meet Katie and the Preservation Society at the Elsie Dyck house. By the time I got there it was late and the sun had already gone down. I parked a block away, not wanting my truck to be seen in the vicinity. When I stepped out onto the flooded pavement, my boots filled with water and I walked down the street like this, with soaking feet, muttering profanities under my breath.

Mr. Wiebe had his headlights shining up at the house, and a Plautdietsch program was playing on his radio. I think it was a comedy, but I wasn't entirely certain about the content since even very serious Plautdietsch programming just sounds funny. It's the way they say it. I told Mr. Wiebe that I could hear the radio from quite a distance. He turned down the volume.

"It's not appropriate content anyway, considering the circumstances," he said.

Mrs. Friesen, however, said it was always a good time to laugh and Elsie Dyck would probably have laughed along with them if she were there. Sheila said she'd just been reading *A Doll's Housebarn* and said there wasn't a single thing to laugh about in that whole book.

"It's utterly devastating," she said.

Mrs. Friesen said there was actually a lot of amusing material in the subtext that Sheila must have missed, being from the city and all, but she promised she wouldn't hold it against her.

"They're inside jokes," she said.

Mr. Wiebe had overdone it on the pickleball court the other day, so his role that evening was to keep everyone's spirits up, keep a lookout for city employees, and hop in the truck with Mr. Harder and fetch us more coffee when we needed it.

"Mr. Harder?" I asked.

I looked in the truck. There he was, thermos in hand.

He gave me a friendly wave. He even had a box of donuts for us.

Mrs. Friesen and Mrs. Ens continued piling up the sandbags they had brought from their own homes to keep the water from entering the building. This was against BLT's strict orders, but Mrs. Friesen said she thought his orders were "about as worthy of my attention as Reverend Broesky's admonishments against card playing."

Mrs. Ens's grandchildren had not shown up. Their parents had not been in favour of their involvement.

"My Gabrielle, such a sweet girl, but she's got no spine at all. I shake my head when I think of how she's raising those kids," said Mrs. Ens. "It's a good thing you're here, though."

She gave me some fresh dry socks, saying she always had an emergency backup pair, then tossed me a sandbag, which I bobbled and dropped. Katie said that if I was feeling uncertain about all this I could take the first position in line.

"That way you're not directly involved," she said.

"What do you mean?"

"You fill the bag and pass it on to me. I'll pass it to Mrs. Ens. She'll pass it to Sheila, who'll pass it to Mrs. Friesen, who'll throw it on the pile. See? You had nothing to do with it. Plausible deniability. Just like all those presidential scandals. If BLT or any of his henchmen show up, just say, 'Well, I don't know. I was just filling the bags and passing them along, and I'm not responsible for what someone else does with it once it's out of my hands.'"

I looked at Mrs. Friesen, her pants tucked into her rubber boots.

"I'd actually like to go to the end of the line if that's okay," I said. I tucked in my pants to match Mrs. Friesen's.

We worked like this all evening, stopping occasionally to make sure our pants were properly tucked. Some water did get in our boots, I'll admit that, but it wasn't too bad and after an hour we were beginning to see some progress. This was aided by the fact that our numbers had grown. I'd been paying so much attention to making sure the house was well protected that I hadn't noticed that a few people had joined our ranks. Dorothy from the library was there. The janitor from South Edenfeld showed up too. I learned that evening that his name was Collin Unrau. Even Old Stuff Timothy locked up the archives and drove out to help us. We made a lot of noise and a lot of progress, but the authorities never showed up and the neighbours, who I suspect might have been in Playa del Carmen, didn't even turn the porch light on. A dog barked for a while, but eventually he shut up after he realized no one was paying much attention to him. By midnight we had a nice wall built around the house.

"It's beautiful," said Sheila.

"That's not the word I'd use to describe it," said Katie, "but it should hold."

When Mrs. Friesen washed the sand off her hands, she noticed they were red and inflamed.

"I should've gone easier," she said, "but I've got some Wonder Oil at home, so I should be okay."

Mrs. Ens pulled Sheila towards her, then got everyone to stand in a row, arms linked, and took a photo of everything we had accomplished. I was impressed that she owned a selfie stick.

"It's just like all those insipid photo ops that BLT likes to take," she said. "Too bad I'll never be able to show this to anyone." Then she shook her head and said she might do it anyway. "What have I got to lose?"

And so we left, each one of us departing to our own houses dirty and exhausted, but feeling buoyed by the fact that the Preservation Society had grown by a few members and finally lived up to its name in some small way. Katie and I traipsed through the water back to our truck and drove home. She fell asleep with her head on my shoulder. The drive was two minutes long.

I suppose that under normal circumstances, our barrier would have withstood most southern Manitoba floods. We had done a good job. We were all quite satisfied that our wall was mostly impermeable, at least to any natural conditions. We couldn't factor in the work of the devil, however, and all it took was one of the Thiessen boys in the middle of the night with a backhoe to spoil our plans. The next morning, when I drove by the house, there were trucks and a reporter from the newspaper interviewing the mayor who said it was sad to see this historic land-mark receive such damage.

"We tried to save it," I heard him say, "but Mother Nature had ideas of her own."

Then he made some reference to the flood of Noah and how God had saved two of every kind of animal so that humanity could start afresh. He even made some veiled reference to baptism. To him, it was yet another story of progress. "Out with the old and in with the new," he said. That was the headline in the town paper.

The house wasn't completely destroyed, but it had

suffered significant damage. When the flood waters subsided a few weeks later, there was still water in the cellar, and the whole thing leaned to one side. The front yard was muddy and there was police tape across the property warning people to keep out, like a murder had taken place. BLT even had us put plywood boards across the windows so "derelicts and raccoons don't try to get in." He said both those things were a very real possibility and made sure the house was padlocked and all the entry points were secured. "We don't want to have the same problem we had with the old Lepp place, remember? These sorts of buildings attract all the wrong people for all the wrong reasons." There hadn't been any issues with the Lepp housebarn, or the Hiebert barn, either, but BLT has this way of creating fictions that become part of the collective memory of our community. "Ah, yes, the Lepp barn. I remember that place. Complete squalor as I recall. Racoon infestation. That fire was a blessing in disguise."

The Preservation Society, which had grown to fifteen people by the next meeting, decided they would counter BLT's stranglehold on the local narrative by giving free Plautdietsch lessons at the library and setting up a local history lecture series. Katie and I were the first to sign up for the language lessons and I must say my ability to eavesdrop on the women in floral dresses below Ernie's increased dramatically. Mr. Wiebe planned to speak on Mennonite architecture through the ages and someone was scheduled to come in from Altfeld to talk about the Schellenberg family gospel quartet, the only one in the region to feature three sopranos and a bass. Some members figured we might even be able to convince Elsie Dyck to come out and speak, but this raised the whole question of her existence and whether, if she did exist, she'd be willing to visit our fair town after what had happened to her former home. Mrs. Friesen said anything was possible, but everyone else thought she was just having one of her flights of fancy again.

# Twenty

Katie's grandmother said we needn't be too concerned about the fact that the Elsie Dyck house had been moved out of town and was now being used as a cowshed. There was nothing wrong with sheltering cattle over by Rosenthal, she said. "That's a perfectly respectable task for an old house." We described how we had tried to save it, had grunted and sweated all evening piling all those sandbags, but when our barrier was sabotaged, the water flowed in and BLT demanded that the building be torn down.

"The only reason it was saved from demolition," Katie explained, "was because some journalist from one of the city papers snapped a photo of the house and slapped it on the front page of the Arts section. Bad press. BLT says the city people are always trying to make us look bad.

To avoid further controversy, BLT sold the house to Mr. Kettler for a dollar."

"Not only that," I said, "but last week someone came and painted a red dot on the big old elm tree in our backyard. I was really hoping they'd ignore it, since it's behind the house and all, but the chainsaws are scheduled to arrive on Friday while we're away."

"I'll miss it," Katie said, "but it's diseased. It needs to go."

Grandma Brandt fed us cheese and baked goods and told us about the poetry recitals in the barn loft she had attended over the winter. There had also been a cello performance by "this woman from somewhere near Fischau with pierced eyebrows." She said that she was a rather talented cellist nonetheless. The whole village, she said, was also looking forward to the horseshoes tournament next week, which was the first one of the season.

Katie showed her grandmother her diploma. Master of Arts (*summa cum laude*). Grandma Brandt hadn't been able to make it to the ceremony. She rarely leaves Altfeld at her age. Katie gave her a copy of her thesis, though, and Grandma Brandt promised she'd read it and give her feedback. "The Phallogocentric Religio-ethnic Culture of Edenfeld, Manitoba." Katie says she's thinking of starting her PhD next semester. "Cultural Hegemony in the Contemporary Mennonite Milieu." That's the tentative idea, anyway.

We played a game of Scrabble without the dictionary and I lost handily. I doubt if I even broke one hundred. Then, after a second game and more cheese, Katie gave her grandma a long hug and a kiss on the cheek and said we had to go and not only because our knowledge of two-letter words had been exhausted. We had a flight to catch.

While we were putting on our shoes, Katie's grandmother asked if a margarine container's worth of meat buns would help tide us over on the drive to the airport. Katie assured her they would.

Grandma Brandt asked how long we'd be out in Russia and we told her we would only be gone three weeks, which wasn't actually so long when you factor in that two days are lost in plane travel and another two each way on the train to and from Omsk. She squeezed us tight and shed a tear as if we were moving away rather than just going for a wedding.

"We'll help you pick rhubarb when we get back," I said. Katie told me later that the rhubarb wouldn't be ready for picking by then.

On our way to the city, we drove past the Elsie Dyck cowshed. Katie thought we didn't have time to stop, but I said the airport always overestimates how early you need to arrive before your departure time. Two hours was overkill, I said, and so we stopped for a moment to watch the cows go in and out of the building a few times. Katie wanted to buy some milk, but we were told there's a law that makes it illegal to buy it directly from a farmer. Instead, all the milk from all the cows in the area gets put in one giant tank and you never know if you're drinking the milk from Elsie Dyck's cows or not.

There wasn't even a sign to straighten, so Katie resigned herself to taking a few pictures. Before we left, I reached into my pocket and pulled out the piece of flooring I'd taken from the wreckage of the Hiebert housebarn. I thought for a second of going out there and laying it down somewhere beside the building, but Katie thought that would be "like casting pearls before swine." She took the piece from me and positioned it on the dashboard to take a picture with the Elsie Dyck house and a few cows in the background. She said she was going to send her photos to Mrs. Friesen for the Society newsletter, the first issue of which is set for publication later in the month. We have over a hundred subscribers already. Katie plans to simplify a few of her essays for publication and Mr. Wiebe and Mrs. Ens also have a few pieces ready to go. The bulk of the material, however, is coming from the nine hundred pages I wrote for the Edenfeld book that never got published. They're planning to serialize it. There are only so many pages that spiral binding can hold, so the group felt it would be better to release the material gradually. "Like a boiling frog," Mrs. Friesen said.

There are also rumours that Elsie Dyck is just about finished a new book, the first one in twelve years. Mrs. Friesen said she'd heard rumblings about it at the mall in the city, but the others had their doubts about the reliability of anything that originated in a food court. I told them to at least reserve their judgment. "I'll err on the side of Mrs. Friesen," I said. I'm pretty excited about an Elsie Dyck comeback novel. *East of Edenfeld* is the title that's going around.

Of course, BLT has already written half a dozen editorials in the local paper discrediting her, saying that she has absolutely no clue what a great place this is now. He's trying to play it up like it's no big deal, but I think he's actually pretty worried about it since the megamart developers have been in town investigating. He said the canonical story of Pretty Plain has already been written "by our very own Timothy Heppner," and nothing more ever needs to be said on the topic. The book—my book—was available, he pointed out, for only fifteen dollars at Frugal Frank's and Ernie's and the Co-op out on the highway. If you fill up your tank and purchase a sausage-scented air freshener, you can get the book for twenty percent off.

I think he's a bit confused, though. "I can't figure it out, Timothy," BLT said. "People are buying your book, but they're just not getting the message." I guess he's noticed that as more copies of that book are sold, the opposition to his plans for Edenfeld grows. People are demanding that the unoccupied lots be sold at fair prices to local people, to small businesses run by Edenfelders. One man wants to start a record store. Another person is opening up one of those oil and vinegar tasting rooms. Some are even having second thoughts about the town's name change and are calling it Edenfeld again, at least in casual conversation. Nevertheless, the mayor is undeterred and wants to make sure the word gets out and the book is "properly understood." They've already done a second printing. They were supposed to do one sooner, but the flood waters kept the trucks that supply our spiral binding away, and when they finally could get through into town, there were plenty of other books that needed binding and mine was put on the backburner since my death was not quite as impending as some of the other authors. They're also expecting me to write a sequel in the same vein as the original called *Pretty Plain: The Undiscovered Country*, which will be followed in rapid succession by a third part called *Pretty Plain: The Wrath of Krahn.*

The numbers are also way up at the Preservation

Society. We had almost twenty people at our last meeting and Mrs. Ens is having trouble baking enough butter tarts. The demand is so high that Mr. Wiebe has tried his hand at baking but thankfully this has not deterred anyone from attending. It would be going too far to say I'm optimistic about things. We've lost a lot of our history and much of it will never be restored, but there's real hope that we can finally get the roof fixed at the library, update the personal computers, maybe expand the selection of books. I was thinking local history. There are hundreds of books in the closets and under the beds in Edenfeld homes. Some are even embossed. Some are spiral-bound. Some are hard-cover. They should all have a place in the library. There will always be things worth fighting for.

So, here we are, still waiting for air traffic control to give the pilot the green light to get this thing off the ground. I've already skimmed through the airline magazine twice and I've given up on the crossword. What's a ten-letter word meaning "acquiescence"?

Katie has already started an old Bette Davis movie while our plane is still on the ground. There's hope, though, because the flight attendant just came by and leaned into our row to lift up the window shade. I was actually hoping for peanuts because we hadn't eaten anything since Grandma Brandt's meat buns in the car on the way to the airport. We got absolutely no refreshments, however, only instructions.

"These have got to stay open during takeoff and

landing," she said, then asked me to move my pillow out of the way so that my seatbelt was clearly visible.

I knew enough to keep my seat in an upright position, which was uncomfortable but useful since the person behind me kept bumping my seat and would have been coughing directly into the back of my neck had I been positioned at any other angle.

We have a connection in Toronto and then Frankfurt and then, once we get to Moscow, Randall said we could either risk it with a Russian airline or take a forty-hour train trip to Omsk where he'd meet us at the station. We've elected for the train, not because we're afraid of the food on Russian airlines, but because we want to see some of those beautiful countryside churches that Mr. Harder told me about. That's the plan, anyway. At the moment, though, we're still just taxiing.

Randall said he and Brenda are in the process of purchasing some land and a small house as close to Last Edenfeld as they can. If all the paperwork goes through, they're hoping to spend the next few years reconstructing the village to the way it was before it was abandoned in the 1930s. They have pretty grand ambitions and I told him my construction skills were quite limited and I would likely not be of much use. He told me not to worry and said he hadn't invited me to put me to work. We were there to see the country and witness their nuptials, and that's it. Plus, Brenda said May was the best time for a destination wedding in Siberia. Apparently, the weather is nice and the flights are a lot cheaper than in peak Omsk tourist season.

I stood up to grab a few snacks from the overhead compartment. Somehow, we were able to get Grandma

Brandt's meat buns through security. I imagine they must have looked completely innocent on the X-ray, like rolled-up nylons or something. When I stood up, I was immediately scolded for my sheer disregard of airplane safety. Thankfully, I managed to scrounge a few meat buns before anyone felt I had violated enough rules to be escorted off the flight.

It seems the plane is about to take off now. They're telling us to put away our electronic devices. Katie's given up on the movie and is snuggling up next to me like she always does during takeoff.

"I prefer gravel roads," she says.

I think I agree, but I don't say it out loud. I tell her I'm planning to do some more writing, maybe start something new, an uncommissioned work of fiction, something truly my own. We have a long flight ahead of us and I've seen *All About Eve* many times before, so I think I'll get started now. I've got a few ideas that I'm eager to get down, once the plane's in the air and I can lower my tray table, that is. I've never written anything like that before, I tell Katie. She smiles and says she's sure I'll do just fine. She asks me not to wake her for the duration of the flight, unless I have a really pressing question about character development or something of that nature, and I promise to keep my inquiries to a minimum. Katie removes her shoes and tucks them under the seat. She rests her head on my shoulder and I kiss the top of her head, this time certain that I'm not disturbing her. Then she closes her eyes and falls asleep while the flight attendant points out the emergency exits and the place where the masks will drop from in case of loss of cabin pressure, and with Katie in my arms, I know

that my new book will go smoothly and I'll probably put
my name on it, and I don't think either of us are the least
bit concerned that we're missing the safety talk.

# Acknowledgements

Apart from the ever-present threat of being called before the church elders, the greatest fear a Mennonite writer has is the guilt and shame that accompanies the inadequate expression of gratitude. After all, we cannot be seen as insufficiently humble. But I guess the safest bet is to keep my acknowledgements rather short and non-specific, so that others can share in this tradition of humility, and also so that I can diminish the risk of having anyone feel left out. I do, however, want to mention a few people by name. In all sincerity, thank you to the amazing folks at Turnstone Press for your work and support at every stage of this project. Thank you to Sarah Ens for your wonderful insight during the substantive editing, and to Melissa McIvor for your keen eye during copyediting and proofing. Thanks also to Margruite Krahn for your work in preserving traditional Mennonite floor patterns and for allowing me to use one of these patterns on the cover of this book.

There are many others—all these unnamed souls—who deserve to be thanked: established writers for your advice, local historians (both amateur and professional) for your knowledge, archivists for showing me around, friends for reading very early versions of this book, Plautdietsch experts for correcting my spelling, family for your support, and *The Daily Bonnet* readers for reading, sharing, and supporting my writing. Thank you, everyone!

Most of all, thank you to my wife and distant cousin Erin, who is many of these things and so much more.